Bolan charged down the hall with a snarl of bullets

Some of his opponents wore body armor, but the M4's deadly sputter struck with enough force to slow them down, allowing Bolan to adjust aim and send rounds into their exposed heads and throats.

Between Rojas's sniping, Bolan's blitz and the gunmen's agitated state, the Soldados de Cali Nuevos didn't stand a chance in this tenement.

It took all of a minute and two thirty-round magazines to completely clear the first story. The second story was alive with breaking glass and screaming. Rojas wasn't allowing the Soldados a moment of respite.

By the time Bolan reached the second-floor corridor, only a few men remained within sight. The Executioner shouldered his rifle and drilled one of them through the side of his head with a single round. The other Soldado let out a scream and waved his machine pistol wildly. In the dark hallway, Bolan was a wraith among the shadows.

"On two," Bolan told Rojas. "Don't shoot me."

"Wouldn't dream of it," she replied. "I'm saving all my ammo and hatred for the enemy."

MACK BOLAN ®
The Executioner

THE EXECUTIONER

DON PENDLETON'S

KILLPATH

A GOLD EAGLE BOOK FROM

W⬤RLDWIDE®

TORONTO • NEW YORK • LONDON
AMSTERDAM • PARIS • SYDNEY • HAMBURG
STOCKHOLM • ATHENS • TOKYO • MILAN
MADRID • WARSAW • BUDAPEST • AUCKLAND

First edition July 2015

ISBN-13: 978-0-373-64440-7

Special thanks and acknowledgment to
Douglas Wojtowicz for his contribution to this work.

Killpath

Recycling programs
for this product may
not exist in your area.

Printed in U.S.A.

Wild animals never kill for sport. Man is the only one to whom the torture and death of his fellow creatures is amusing in itself.

—James Anthony Froude,
1818–1894

I take no pleasure in ending a life, but I will not hesitate to deliver the ultimate punishment in the name of justice. Those who willfully inflict suffering on others must pay the price.

—Mack Bolan

THE
MACK BOLAN
LEGEND

Nothing less than a war could have fashioned the destiny of the man called Mack Bolan. Bolan earned the Executioner title in the jungle hell of Vietnam.

But this soldier also wore another name—Sergeant Mercy. He was so tagged because of the compassion he showed to wounded comrades-in-arms and Vietnamese civilians.

Mack Bolan's second tour of duty ended prematurely when he was given emergency leave to return home and bury his family, victims of the Mob. Then he declared a one-man war against the Mafia.

He confronted the Families head-on from coast to coast, and soon a hope of victory began to appear. But Bolan had broken society's every rule. That same society started gunning for this elusive warrior—to no avail.

So Bolan was offered amnesty to work within the system against terrorism. This time, as an employee of Uncle Sam, Bolan became Colonel John Phoenix. With a command center at Stony Man Farm in Virginia, he and his new allies—Able Team and Phoenix Force—waged relentless war on a new adversary: the KGB.

But when his one true love, April Rose, died at the hands of the Soviet terror machine, Bolan severed all ties with Establishment authority.

Now, after a lengthy lone-wolf struggle and much soul-searching, the Executioner has agreed to enter an "arm's-length" alliance with his government once more, reserving the right to pursue personal missions in his Everlasting War.

Mack Bolan, the Executioner, slipped into the shadows, gliding slowly through the night, scarcely disturbing the surrounding foliage.

He was armed for a soft probe tonight. A Drug Enforcement Agency operative had gone missing, and he was searching for her on this small Texas estate. While more conventional law enforcement would take at least a couple of days to seek out the agent, Hal Brognola knew that the Executioner's touch was exactly what was needed to dig her out of the fire.

Bolan moved with the stealth of a black panther, despite the forty pounds of gear stashed in his combat harness and the pockets of his blacksuit.

He did not merely blend in with the shadows; he was one, flowing across the property with fluid grace and silence until he was only a few feet from a guard. Behind the man, Bolan was in a good position to take stock of the rest of the estate's security. From his approach, and from viewing the area with a night vision monocle, he could tell the place was mobbed up to the gills. The guard in front of him wore night vision goggles and was packing serious firepower, an M4 carbine equipped with various optics and grips. It was an impressive setup, but it was an obvious case of the guard putting everything he thought was cool onto his personal rifle. Even now, the guy was fidgeting with the unnecessary weight.

Bolan wished he could have given this tyro a chance to learn from his mistakes, but the sentry was armed, and he was currently pulling guard duty on an estate where a kidnapped federal agent was held captive. This man was willing to kill, even if he was too heavily burdened to do it efficiently. With a swift movement, Bolan brought a loop of inelastic polymer wire down over the guard's head and yanked on the handles. The wire sliced through skin as if it were butter, crushing down on the tough, fibrous tube of the man's windpipe. The garrote would take a little more effort to cut into his trachea, but for now, the guard was unable to speak, which was a fine start in silently removing him from his post.

Bolan dragged him back into the trees at the edge of the property. The man grasped at the wire and his hands came away covered in crimson liquid. The polymer dug deeper and was now embedded at least an inch into the guard's throat. Bolan was not someone to let a man suffer, so he pulled down hard, breaking the mobster's neck on the point of his Kevlar polymer knee guard.

Fast. Silent. Relatively merciful. The warrior tucked the body beneath a patch of bushes, leaving the wire garrote around the dead man's neck. There was no way he could untangle the weapon without spattering himself with blood, and the scent of gore was something that carried and could compromise this operation.

Speed and stealth were the Executioner's priorities tonight. Overwhelming firepower from the start would only endanger the captive agent and draw the law into this. Bolan hoped that this wouldn't become a recovery instead of a rescue. Still, he was well-equipped for any situation that might arise. Aside from various means of silent death in the form of impact weapons, garrotes and knives, he packed his traditional sidearm, the Beretta 93R machine pistol.

For backup and long-range engagements when stealth might no longer be a factor, he wore his Desert Eagle .44 Magnum on his hip in a fast-draw holster. This would be his last resort. Bolan decided to leave the dead guard's rifle behind, though he swiftly removed the magazine and the bolt, rendering it useless.

Along with his blacksuit, Bolan wore crepe-soled boots, which would make little sound as he crept along. He'd smeared his hands and face with black greasepaint, completing his transformation from soldier to shadowy wraith. This was as much for the intimidation factor as for blending in with the darkness.

More than once, the Executioner's jet-black mien had been sufficient to freeze a group of opponents in shock and horror long enough for him to outgun them. If he were going for pure camouflage, he would have donned multiple shades of gray, which would help him merge even more seamlessly with the shadows. But midnight-black would have a much stronger psychological impact on anyone crossing his path. So far, he hadn't been detected. If someone did see him, Bolan would have a short window of opportunity in which his foe would be struggling to recover from the shock of the shadow man's apparition.

The disappearance of DEA operative Teresa Blanca would not have normally drawn the Executioner down to this part of the country within a day of her first failure to report in, but she had been undercover in an effort to break Los Soldados Nuevos de Cali, a rising force not only in Colombia, but also with tentacles stretching out across Central America and latching on to the soft underbelly of the United States. The New Soldiers of Cali had been little more than a blip on the radar five years before, but in the intervening time, they had proven themselves to be ruthless and powerful fighters.

The details on SNC were sketchy at best, but as far as the Executioner could tell, the organization was using a combination of military planning, technol-

ogy and unconventional warfare to enrich themselves
and maintain an ironclad control over their territory
and the products they trafficked.

Blanca had found her way into the SNC and
had been sending back some good intel before she
popped up in Brownsville, Texas. That was a bad
thing since she was supposed to be operating in Cali,
Colombia, thousands of miles south. She'd sent off
one message, and then nothing.

That was ten hours ago. Her panicked support in
Cali confirmed that she'd gone to America on a pri-
vate flight. Border Control hadn't seen any hint of
her arrival on US soil.

Bolan, already on the Texas Gulf Coast doing
some pre-mission observation of a Zetas operation,
had picked up a rumor that the Mexican cartel was
working with the SNC. It made sense for the two
paramilitary units to form an alliance rather than
engage in warfare with each other. Granted, both
parties would be looking out for themselves, but for
now, there was cooperation.

Cooperation, including the captivity of a woman
trying to uphold the law.

Keeping both hands free and moving in a low and
easy crouch, the Executioner crept along in the darkness. He was confident he could avoid most of the
opposition without a hint of trouble, now that he'd
removed the sole sentry who would have noticed his
chosen approach to the mansion. Still, shifts could
be changing, and there was always the risk of a wan-

dering eye picking up his movements. So far, his instincts had been solid, but he paused to double-check his surroundings.

The Zetas security force still moved according to the pattern Bolan had observed earlier. Satisfied, Bolan continued his advance, and within a moment, he was at the small enclosure surrounding the garbage bins. Using the structure for cover, he did a quick eyeball of the camera trained on the kitchen entrance. He pulled out a small device, aimed and sent an electromagnetic pulse toward the surveillance equipment, turning the electronics inside of the camera housing into so much useless scrap. With the back of the house no longer under a live eye, Bolan took off for the kitchen door. Along the way, he traded the camera-killer for a SWAT-style pry-knife.

With one hand, Bolan tried the door handle. If it was unlocked, no problem. If it *was* locked, the chisel-like blade would punch out the latch in a second. The handle caught, so Bolan jammed the pry-knife between the door and the frame until he had sufficient leverage to burst the latch.

There was a loud crack, and then the door swung open. Bolan stepped inside the mansion. The sound was likely to draw attention, but no one would have mistaken it for a gunshot. There would be no sudden, armed response.

This conflict was still contained.

Bolan slid into the shadows of a large pantry as a man entered the kitchen, his eyes on the fridge. The lights were off, and the refrigerator's glow cast the man in silhouette. This wasn't a casual homeowner. Not too many homeowners, even in Texas, went to get a midnight snack with a semiautomatic shotgun on a three point sling with a full bandolier of shells.

Bolan moved quickly, clamping a blackened hand over the man's nose and mouth, causing him to stiffen reflexively. He tried to grab Bolan's forearm and wrist as the Executioner plunged the flat edge of the pry-knife into the base of the man's skull. Flesh, tendon and cartilage parted under the force of his stab. Any attempt at struggle on the part of the guard was instantly over.

Bolan lowered the body to the floor, pulling it behind the central counter island. For the moment, the lifeless hardman would be out of sight and out of mind.

Bolan inched toward the kitchen doorway that led to the rest of the house, using a pocket mirror to check the hall in both directions before passing through it. He unholstered the suppressed Beretta and made for the closest staircase. Before he reached it, he heard the sounds of a soccer game and excited but hushed voices wafting from a television nearby.

"Eh, Chuy! *Donde estan los cervezas?*" a man said in a stage whisper just before a figure filled the TV room doorway.

The man asking for the beer froze, eyes wide at the sight of the Executioner, ebony from head to toe, bristling with weapons on his battle harness, and a handgun pointed right at him. At once frightened and confused, the man was paralyzed, buying the warrior a precious second.

Bolan stabbed the Beretta and its suppressor between the man's lips, then grabbed the back of his neck and whisked him away from the TV room and into the empty hallway.

"The girl," Bolan said softly, his voice full of grim threat.

The Zeta swiveled his eyes and shook his head in the direction of the stairs.

Bolan delivered a powerful knuckle punch just under the Zeta's ear. Pulling the trigger would have alerted the men watching *futbol* to the death of their friend, and stabbing the guy could lead to a struggle that would also draw his companions into the hall. A knockout punch, however, would be both silent and disabling. The man's knees turned to rubber, and Bolan dragged him over to an empty closet at the foot of the stairs, tucking him inside. So far, so good.

Bolan continued to the second floor, feet quiet on the steps and Beretta drawn. It was do-or-die time, and if he needed to pull the trigger, he'd have the high ground in case anyone heard the thump of a silenced 9mm slug erupting from the machine pistol. He'd do whatever it took to defend Blanca.

Or avenge her.

As much as Bolan wanted to dismiss that possibility, Blanca had been a prisoner of the Zetas, as well as the Soldados. These cartels weren't known for their mercy. They might have tortured and executed her already, but there was a shred of hope. The guard he'd just knocked out hadn't hesitated when Bolan had asked after the "girl." Hopefully that meant Blanca was somewhere upstairs. Alive. Unless there was another girl in this house…

A man wearing no shirt but with a gun holstered at his hip emerged from a bedroom and stepped smugly into Bolan's path. Catching sight of the Executioner, the guy's smirk faltered, but his reflexes were better than his colleague's and his hand went to his pistol.

Bolan was faster, though, and the Beretta chugged three times. The slugs penetrated the man's bare chest, and he crashed into the door, knocking it open as he slithered lifelessly to the ground.

Bolan heard a confused yelp from inside the bedroom and saw a shadow move across the floor.

"Quién es—"

Bolan charged across the threshold, lunging over the body. The man inside was also half-dressed, but he'd managed to snatch his weapon off the floor and aim it at the intruder. The Executioner sent the man off to his final damnation with a heart-coring second burst. He crumpled against a small desk.

There was a woman curled up on the bed, her shoulders shuddering as she sobbed. Whatever had happened in here before Bolan arrived, she obviously hadn't been a willing participant.

At least those two sickos couldn't do her any more harm, Bolan thought grimly.

But this was not Agent Blanca.

Bolan heard movement on the first floor, heading in his direction. He'd given away his presence, and his mission was far from complete. And now he had to figure out how to keep this woman out of the line of fire.

All before his enemies reached the top of the stairs.

2

With a strong hand, Bolan pulled the crying woman to her feet. Her eyes were red, and her movements were dull and confused, but after an initial squeak of panic, she seemed to realize that Bolan wasn't going to hurt her.

He pushed her toward the closet.

"Stay in there and tuck yourself into the corner," Bolan said. She slid inside, then quickly pulled the door closed.

It was time to go loud. Bolan plucked a flash-bang grenade from his combat harness, hurling it into the hallway so it bounced down the steps after a skillful rebound. The canister detonated amidst the group rushing toward him.

After the explosion had subsided, Bolan scooped up a Kalashnikov and a bandolier from the man he'd taken out in the bedroom and darted into the hall to assess the situation. Four men stood on the landing below, each clutching their eyes or ears. At such close range, the blast would have been strong enough to rupture eardrums. Bolan scanned past the staggering guards. Not much movement down there, so he returned his attention to the landing.

The sentries had guns, and soon they'd recover their wits and eyesight enough to open fire.

Bolan shouldered the stock of the Kalashnikov and pumped hot lead at the group, the sharp crack of the rifle informing him that this was a 5.45 mm caliber AK, not the 7.62. Even so, at this range, the high-velocity projectiles slashed through human flesh and shattered bone as they struck.

It was brutal, but these men would overwhelm him with handgun and machine pistol fire in seconds if he let them. And now Bolan wasn't just looking out for himself. The girl who'd tucked herself into the closet only had drywall for protection, and drywall was poor cover against high-velocity bullets.

With half of the magazine from the AK used, Bolan slapped out the spent box, picking up another from a bandolier that the dead man in the doorway wore. Once the firearm was fully loaded, *then* the Executioner spent a moment tugging the belt of spare mags off of the corpse. Bolan paused to reload. By his estimation, the guard force outside the house would have heard the gunfire, and it would take them about half a minute to enter the building, if that. The most aggressive men would be bursting through the doors now, but cooler heads would not want to rush into a building with an unknown enemy inside.

That meant he could expect two waves, one full of hot-blooded young bucks, the second a more cautious and experienced group. Bolan kept his ears open for the initial approach, which would be anything but quiet. Now, he had precious seconds to look through the other rooms along this corridor before returning to the bottleneck at the top of the stairs.

Bolan swept into each bedroom, scanning for any sign of Teresa Blanca. He got to the end of the hallway without finding her, then the sound of men climbing the stairs forced him to direct his attention back to the enemy. The warrior took cover behind a doorjamb, making himself as small a target as possible. He had a clear line of fire against his opposition, as long as they poked their heads over the top of the stairs.

The first of the gunmen rose up, and Bolan let him go for a few moments. Another guy popped up behind him and covered his partner. The Executioner cut them both down, short tri-bursts punching their bodies sideways.

Screams resounded from behind and below them as their corpses toppled on to others. Bolan continued shooting, raking the air just over the top step. High-velocity slugs smashed through the faces that popped into view.

Curses filled the air, and, as if on cue, a wave of gunfire whipped down the hall toward Bolan. Bullets tore into the ceiling and walls, but none came close to touching him. Still, he wasn't about to sit back and watch the proceedings. Bolan threw a flash-bang grenade off the far wall, and it rebounded down the corridor in a well-planned trajectory.

Instants later, the distraction device detonated with the force of a thunderbolt. Bolan exploded into the hall, keeping low and covering distance quickly with long strides. He'd reloaded the AK with a fresh magazine, and now he hammered a swath of death and destruction into the Zetas on the stairs.

Bodies writhed as 5.45 mm rounds cartwheeled through flesh. The hapless gunmen fell backward on to the landing in a gory heap. When there were no men left standing and fighting, Bolan slung his rifle and mounted the rail. Swinging his legs over, he slid down past the landing, then hopped back on to the staircase below the pile of thugs.

"Es peligroso aquí!" Bolan shouted loud enough for the woman in the closet to hear. *"No se mueva!"*

"Si!" she responded.

She'd survived in her hideout, and she'd stay put long enough. Satisfied, Bolan continued through the house. If Agent Blanca wasn't on the first or second floors, then she'd be in the basement.

He reloaded as he walked, discarding the spent magazine in the AK, but he returned it to its sling over his shoulder. If he cut loose with the automatic rifle in the close quarters of a basement, he'd end up deafening himself. He switched to the suppressed Beretta instead.

He found the entry to the basement and descended the stairs quickly, but with caution. He didn't want to get caught by a spray of bullets from below, but he wasn't about to wait around for the next wave of guards to show.

The basement was well-lit, but the uneasy silence of the subterranean layout set his instincts on edge. If there was a prisoner, there would be guards. And if there were guards, then his appearance should have elicited a response.

Maybe they were part of the crew that he'd just taken out, but something told him that any hope of rescuing Teresa Blanca was gone. He spotted a hanging sheet of translucent plastic and moved toward it.

No, Blanca no longer required gunmen at the doorway to keep her prisoner. He pushed aside the rubbery drape and stepped into the slaughterhouse.

Blanca's forehead sported a still-smoking bullet hole, and the rest of her body showed signs of recent and brutal torture.

There was a muffled sound in the corner of the room. Bolan turned and saw a couple of disposal bins. As he walked closer, a muzzle rose shakily from behind one of them. The barrel of a pistol came into view, but Bolan had sidestepped from in front of the gun. He reached over the top of the gun's slide and clamped down, twisting the weapon loose from the hand holding it with the snap of finger bones. A man cried out, recoiling and kicking one of the canisters aside.

A man in a white coat held his hand gingerly, his trigger finger broken by the Executioner's disarm.

"Was that Teresa Blanca?" Bolan asked.

The man was in his late forties, his wet hair matted across a receding hairline near the top of his skull. He was drenched with sweat. His big, trembling lips sputtered for a few moments. "Yes. It was her."

"And you shot her?" Bolan asked.

The man gave a jerky nod. "Yes. I heard the gunfire upstairs…"

"What about the torture?" Bolan pressed. "Were you part of that, too?"

"Please. I stopped her suffering. Don't hurt me." He swallowed hard. "I was just following orders."

Bolan pressed a small handgun, a .22 auto-back, into the man's hand, squeezing his fingers around the weapon. "I won't hurt you."

The torturer blinked.

"Take off the lab coat," Bolan barked.

"W-why…"

"Because you'll be too easy to spot," Bolan said. "You don't want to get shot, do you?"

The man quickly began peeling off his coat. "You think there will still be shooting?"

Bolan heard footsteps on the stairs he'd just come down. The second wave was here, and part of the group had been dispatched to the basement.

"Over there!" Bolan shouted. He brought up his big Desert Eagle from its hip holster. As if spurred on, the torturer raised his own tiny pistol, shooting through the plastic tarp hanging in the doorway before the Executioner could even pull the trigger.

Bolan cut loose with the .44 Magnum to make certain that the Zetas gunmen had something to focus on. The room filled with flying lead, bullets cutting through the walls and plastic alike. Bolan threw himself to the ground. The lab coat guy, however, was not so fast to react.

Rifle slugs chopped into his chest, throwing him back over the bins he'd been hiding behind earlier. He reached toward Bolan, fingers stretching and clawing for mercy.

"Physician, heal thyself," the Executioner said.

He brought up the Beretta 93R and cut loose, the silencer smothering any telltale flicker from the sleek machine pistol. He focused on one of the enemy muzzle flashes, and suppressed slugs hit one of the gunmen in the head. The other opponent continued blasting away, but he was on the move, trying not to make himself an easy target.

Bolan blew out the guy's knee with another triburst, and he fell to the ground. The rifle clattered across the floor. The man scrambled to remove his sidearm from its holster, but Bolan stopped him in the act, sending a trio of bullets into the sentry's skull.

The gunfire had drawn more guards to the basement, and they sent two grenades down the steps ahead of them. Bolan supported Teresa Blanca's body with one arm and flipped the steel table with the other. He crouched behind the shrapnel-proof barrier as sheets of shell fragments and notched wire clanged off its surface.

Bolan lowered Blanca to the floor gently. He sent a quiet prayer to the universe to watch over her spirit, and reloaded the Beretta.

Bolan kept the machine pistol handy as he grabbed his last banger from his harness and pulled the pin, counting down as the fuse burned. When the time was right, he dropped the grenade into the middle of the group of guards who'd followed their own bombs down the stairs. Bolan released a loud bellow, equalizing the internal and external pressure on his ears to protect himself from the sound of the explosion.

Bolan rose from behind the steel table and stepped through the shredded plastic sheet. Blinded and deafened foes staggered helplessly around the room. The Executioner lived up to his name, putting bullets into the brains of the trio of Zetas guards directly in front of him. He holstered the machine pistol and pulled out the AK.

.A sentry to the right of him was leaning against a wall, pressing his forearm against his eyes in an effort to restore his burned-out vision. Bolan sliced him in half with a burst from the AK, then turned and spotted another man, blinking and raising his rifle one-handed to gun him down. Bolan sidestepped, aimed the AK with both hands, and tore open the gunman from crotch to throat.

Bolan headed toward the staircase, doing the math on the diminished guard force. There would be two men left at most, plus the guy he'd left unconscious in the hall closet.

His AK was low on ammo, so he drew his Desert Eagle from his hip holster. The door at the top of the stairs was closed—the perfect spot for a gunman to wait him out. Bolan dumped the current magazine in the .44 Magnum and slid in a stick of copper-solid hunting bullets. Pure homogenous copper from nose to tail, these slugs were meant to penetrate the heaviest hides in nature. For the Executioner's purpose, they would tear through walls easily, while causing massive destruction to human flesh.

He loaded the magazine, racked the slide and put the first heavyweight round into the barrel. He paused to scoop up the conventional hollow point and pocket it, not wanting to waste his ammunition. Then he fired two shots through the drywall on either side of the door. The high speed slugs struck and plowed through the plaster, their mass and velocity preventing any deflection. Bolan heard a scream as a man on the other side was hit.

A second guy kicked the door open, and Bolan put a round right into his opponent's rifle. The gun shattered in the man's grasp, saving his life, for the moment. Bolan continued up the stairs as another figure staggered into view. It was the man he'd clobbered before, and he'd rearmed himself.

Another stroke of the Desert Eagle's trigger, and the Executioner all but beheaded him, the copper slug destroying the man's jaw and blasting out the bottom of his skull. By the time the soldier reached the top of the steps, the man who'd lost his rifle had raced out of the kitchen, leaving the back door bouncing on its frame.

The first man, who'd screamed as Magnum slugs tore through the wall and then into his body, lay on the ground, curled up and gasping, blood spurting from his neck. Bolan shot a single copper slug into his brain to end his suffering.

With all of the estate's guards down for the count, Bolan paused to reload his mostly spent weapons, then pulled out his combat PDA. It was time to call Brognola, to let him know the fate of the missing agent. A corpse wagon—several—would be needed for the bodies left sprawled around the property. They would also need an ambulance to recover and treat the woman upstairs. Without Blanca to rescue, only retrieve, the other woman took top priority.

And once she was cared for, the brutal thugs who sent Teresa Blanca to die by the inch were going to dominate the Executioner's attention until every last one of them was dead.

3

Brunhilde Rojas's feet slapped the wet tiles in the prison shower. She admired her taut muscles as she ran the hard, coarse bar of soap over them. Though she was closing in on her fifties, seven years in prison had given her time to maintain a lean and firm body.

Not that Rojas had worked in the prison weight yard for her looks. She kept her body strong for the sake of survival and the hope that maybe, in ten to fifteen years, when she was released, she'd have a chance to get revenge against the bastards who'd killed her boys.

It was a long shot, Rojas admitted to herself as the hot water splashed down on her, matting her inch-long black tresses to her scalp. The spatter of droplets on her skin and on the tile almost drowned out the sound of footsteps behind her.

"Don't drop the soap, Hilda!" came a husky, slurred voice. Chuckles accompanying the speaker's own simplistic tittering confirmed to Rojas that she was outnumbered.

She didn't stop the shower as she turned to face the trio. The speaker, the leader of this group of women, was two inches taller than Rojas, an even six feet. However, this woman was as wide as two of her. The others were slightly smaller than their leader.

Despite Rojas's strength, these women had at least seventy-five pounds on her—each. They were dressed in their orange coveralls, rubber-soled canvas sneakers giving them some traction on the slippery shower floor. Their calloused fists were mute testimony to their experience bludgeoning people.

Rojas didn't say anything, and Pequita Morales cracked her knuckles, smirking at each of her minions in turn.

"Don't worry, Hilda," Morales taunted. "We'll leave your face alone so you can have an open casket funeral."

That was all Rojas needed to hear. She squirted the water she'd trapped in her mouth, hitting Morales in the eyes. Rojas slipped off her shower sandals to get more traction from her bare feet, but she needed to get to the high ground. As Morales brought her hands to her face to protect her splashed eyes, Rojas grabbed on to one of the woman's big, muscular forearms and swung her knee up into the pillowy gut of the hired bruiser. The sudden blow made Morales step backward, pushing her two partners aside and dragging Rojas with her. The naked woman kicked out to her right, the sole of her foot slapping hard into the cheek and jaw of one of the other brawlers. A screech escaped the woman's lips as she staggered back.

Rojas pivoted on her heel and delivered a kick to Morales's sternum. With the speed and lithe power of a leopard, she then brought her elbow into the side of the second minion's neck. Pudgy but powerful arms wrapped around Rojas's shoulders, squeezing her tight and propelling her toward the second bruiser, who was now baring her teeth. Rojas tucked her chin against her chest at the last second. She winced as her opponent's incisors sliced her scalp before they snapped off against her skull.

The grappler let go of Rojas, and the naked woman dropped back to her feet. Her most recent opponent was pouring blood from mashed lips and gums. Morales lunged forward again, having recovered quickly from the blow to her chest. Rojas brought up her elbow in a swift scythe, meeting Morales's face with a crunch. Rojas was knocked off balance as the big woman threw her hands up to her own face. She lost her footing on the slippery floor and hit the tiles. Within seconds, the rubber sole of a sneaker smashed into her ribs.

It was the woman she'd swatted in the face with her bare foot, giving Rojas what she'd paid.

Rojas lashed out and snagged the witch's ankle before she could pull her foot away.

"Puta!" the attacker spat, hopping and windmilling her arms in an effort to stay on her feet. Eventually, Rojas's leverage and gravity won out, and the woman slammed to the ground.

Using every ounce of control in her strong limbs, Rojas rolled on to all fours despite the slickness of the tiles. Two hands clamped on to her neck, hauling her up. Rojas let herself be lifted, feigning weakness as she prepared for her next move. Suddenly, the fingers around her neck let go, and she fell face-first to the floor. She grunted, stunned by the drop.

Morales stomped hard on Rojas's shoulder, and she wanted to cry out in pain. She tried to push up off of the floor when something crashed heavily on to her arm and shoulder. Again her face struck the tiles, blurring her vision and jarring her jaw.

Morales's bulging forearm pushed across her face, and Rojas kept her chin pinned to her clavicle. If that hunk of muscle and power got across her windpipe, everything would be over. Jagged nails stabbed at her forehead, raking back in an effort to wrench her head up.

"Don't struggle so much, Hilda," Morales sneered. "It won't hurt for—"

Rojas lunged up with her good arm, blindly digging her fingers into Morales's meaty face. She jabbed her eye with a thumbnail, and Morales let out a howl. "Enough!"

Heavy boots stomped across the wet tiles. Rojas felt rough hands grip her own trying to make her release Morales's face. Rojas grit her teeth, resisting the guard's efforts. Morales had come after her, taunted her, given her the desire to kill.

She wanted to ensure Morales would never forget her failure to end the life of Brunhilde Rojas. The memory would be scrawled across her face in the unmistakable signature of Rojas's claw marks.

A punch connected with Rojas's jaw, and the world went black.

It had been a good run, but her sons would go unavenged, she thought as she descended into oblivion.

When Rojas opened her eyes, she was dressed. She was in a pair of coveralls, though one of her arms was hanging in a sling under the open front of the prison jumpsuit. She was in an office with a window that showed the open sky outside. She spotted the guard tower nearby. So, she was still on prison property. The desk was clean—no papers, but more importantly, no pens or letter openers that she could grab and turn into a weapon.

A burly man sat in the chair behind the desk, and a tall, dark stranger stood, arms folded, against the wall. Rojas blinked, lingering on the man's cool blue eyes. He was observing her, his features impassive. His presence in the room was a weight, a magnet for her.

"Brunhilde Rojas, aka La Brujah," the seated man

read from a file. "Born in Argentina, daughter of a Colombian father and a German mother, hence the name Brunhilde. Naturalized citizen of the United States at age four."

Rojas glanced at the man behind the desk. He was a broad, serious fellow who showed a road map of years on his face. "So you know who I am…"

"You followed in the footsteps of the Cocaine Godmother and the Queen of the Pacific, right down to having your teenaged sons follow you into the business," the man continued.

"And who are you?" Rojas asked, anger spiking in her voice. Her teenaged sons. *Mis hijos.*

"My name is Harold Brognola, Justice Department," he offered. "And my associate, here, is Matt Cooper."

Rojas's lip twitched. "You mention my sons again…"

"Not even your last remaining son?" Brognola asked.

"Pepito?" Suddenly the iron that was holding her straight in her chair buckled under the weight of her youngest boy's mention. "What have you done with him?"

"We haven't done anything with him other than put him into protective custody," Cooper told her. "But we have found out that your cartel *is* looking for Pepito."

Rojas grit her teeth. "So you come to prison to mock me with this? I've been in a cell for seven years! I don't know anything new."

"Apparently you know enough," Cooper told her. "They sent someone to kill you."

"That didn't work too well for them," Rojas answered.

"You're not an angel," Cooper said. "Not with the dozens of kills you allegedly had a hand in. But you are a mother, and Pedro Rojas *is* innocent."

She leveled her gaze on the blue-eyed, deep-voiced man. He was wearing a short-sleeved shirt, and she could see the powerful swell of muscles, as well as the crisscross of old scars which wove its own tale of a long and brutal life. "So I talk, and then what? You make some arrests, a few men get taken off the streets in New York or in Austin or—"

"Cali." Cooper cut her off.

"You want me to give you information about Cali?" Rojas asked. "It's been a few years since I've been there. Says so right in that file."

"I want more than information," Cooper said. "And I don't want information for arrests. Los Soldados de Cali Nuevos could care less if a few of their guys go to jail. Arrests won't give them a reason to spare Pepito. We need to make them know that even looking at an American citizen again will bring down all the fires of heaven and hell."

Rojas sat back. "No arrests?"

"You still know how to use a gun," Cooper told her. "And while that shoulder is healing up, I'll refresh your skills."

"How bad is my arm?" Rojas asked, looking down

at the poor limb in its sling. Her ribs hurt, too, but at least she could breathe, meaning that they hadn't been broken. "X-rays are still being developed, but it's probably just a dislocated shoulder," Brognola said.

Rojas glanced sideways at Cooper. "And you're going to give me a pistol?"

"Pistols. Rifles. Shotguns. Sub guns. Whatever we need," Cooper answered. "And we're not going to give them to you in here."

Rojas flexed her hand, then gingerly tried to move her arm under the jumpsuit. No, nothing was broken, and Cooper was right; it wouldn't take long for her to get back into fighting condition.

"Why would you help me in protecting my son from the New Soldiers?" Rojas asked. "What do you get out of this?"

"What's in it for us is the same as what's in this for you. Payback," Cooper said. "They killed your sons. They also tortured and killed a DEA agent."

Rojas frowned.

"I'm not asking you to give a damn about Agent Blanca," Cooper continued. "But I do want you to get me close enough to teach the survivors a lesson."

"Survivors," Rojas repeated. She locked eyes with Brognola. "I thought you said you were Justice Department."

"I said I was," Brognola answered. "He didn't."

Rojas pushed herself up from her chair. "And what if I don't want to go?"

Cooper tapped the file in front of Brognola. "The federal government couldn't convict you on the sixty to seventy murders of rivals and fellow gang members you either did yourself or farmed out to hit men. You outsmarted them on that front, so they nailed you on possession and sale of narcotics. But you've got bodies piled up behind you. A lot of bodies."

"You're not appealing to my angels?" Rojas asked.

Cooper narrowed his eyes and stepped closer to her. Their faces were inches apart, and this close, his gaze bored into her. "I'm asking for you to let your devils out to play. So, does the Witch, La Brujah, ride again?"

"If we succeed, what else happens?" Rojas asked.

"Pepito will be safe. And we can fake your death. No one will ever see you again, unless it's on a *telenovella*," Cooper promised.

"I'll be with Pepito?"

Cooper nodded. "I will do everything in my power to make sure you and he are together."

Rojas didn't flinch from his steely gaze. Some voice at the back of her mind brought up the possibility that her Pepito was already dead, and once this was done, this man would put a bullet in the back of her skull.

But these men didn't seem duplicitous. She sensed honesty and strength in Cooper, that made her want to jump at this chance. He didn't seem like a fanatic so much as a crusader, a too-good-to-be-true idealist out to make the world a better place, despite the lethal intentions of going to Cali, armed to the teeth.

"This isn't a trick?" Rojas asked.

"You'll find I'm pretty devious when I'm on the hunt," Cooper said. "But when it comes to making a deal—making an ally—I'm honest. I'm solid. I will go to bat for you."

"Will you take a bullet for me?" Rojas asked.

Cooper took a deep breath. "If you prove yourself as an ally, sure. But I'm not expecting a miracle."

"Because I'm a woman? Because I'm Colombian?"

"Because you've got over sixty dead bodies to your name," he answered.

"How many do you have to yours, Cooper?" The tall, dark man smirked.

"How many?" Rojas pressed.

The way Cooper avoided the question made the hairs on the back of Rojas's neck stand on end.

4

Rojas and Cooper were sitting in business class together, bound for Cali. The only things in their lug-
gage were the standard clothing and toiletries, and
they each had a smartphone in a hard case. Lack of
guns, even a hidden boot knife, made Rojas feel very
bare, like a raw, exposed nerve ready to be plucked.
Cooper didn't seem as anxious; he simply sat back,
studying files on the phone.

Within a day of meeting Cooper and Brognola,
Rojas had gotten rid of the accursed sling. Sure, she
was chewing ibuprofen tablets as if they were breath
mints, but she'd regained full range of motion a day
after that, and the kick of an Uzi's steel folding stock
against her shoulder while on full auto was now completely tolerable.

During their training sessions, Cooper had
watched over her, his gaze wary but not hostile. That

didn't mean he had many smiles for her. Whoever this guy was, he wasn't here to make friends.

The truth hung over the two of them. Rojas had never been a gentle soul, and while she was still enraged at the deaths of her sons, she'd killed their fathers, killed rivals, killed the wives and children of others who dared oppose her as she ran New York City. Cooper had lowballed the number of dead to her name that day in the office, whether by ignorance or by choice.

Even so, he was obviously aware of her past as a ruthless killer. Not that he seemed afraid of her. He was cautious, alert, but Rojas had the impression that one ounce of antagonism toward him would end with her neck snapped.

In the days that had followed their initial meeting, Cooper had re-familiarized her with shooting skills, but he had also taught her the hand signals they would need to work side by side in the field. If he intended to take her life, he would not be such a completist when it came to going into action.

He had made no bones about their plan.

Hilde Rojas was to be the bait. Once she appeared on the scene in Colombia, the SNC would pick up her scent and come after her.

Los Soldados were from a different group than her, another faction of the splintered Colombian drug scene. The old Cali and Medellin cartels were not friends, and much blood had been spilled at the height of their rivalry. When their boss died in a hail of gunfire from a military and police strike, Medellin collapsed into its own mayhem. Nobody there would consider Rojas anything more than a relic of the past.

That she was out of jail after serving only seven of her twenty years would surprise those bosses in Medellin struggling to build a new power base, but she wouldn't draw their attention.

Only the SNC would be interested in La Brujah.

"You also have barely touched your drink," Rojas commented, too restless now to stay silent. "I've got you figured out, you know. You're a professional, and you believe in being in control."

"In control of my thoughts and body," Cooper replied. "I prefer to be aware and at the top of my game. True control of events around you is an illusion."

Rojas thought of her own downfall. For over a decade, she'd smashed all opposition or dissent to her rule with ruthless efficiency. Back then, she'd thought she'd been in total control. The truth was that, eventually, her own people turned against her, flipping on her before she could flip on them. Her wildest *caballeros* had realized that she'd orchestrated so many deaths for the smallest slights or offenses that they themselves could become her next targets.

That was how the DEA had caught her. Someone in her ranks had snitched, but not wanting to implicate themselves in any killings, they'd fed the DEA information about her drug stashes.

Two years of pretrial maneuverings and her conviction meant that she'd missed out on seven of her youngest son's twelve years. Her last living son, and she hadn't been present for more than half of his life.

All because she thought she had more control than she truly did.

"You all right?" Cooper asked.

Rojas nodded. "Why shouldn't I be?"

"You wandered off for a moment."

"Si," Rojas returned. "I'm fine."

Cooper frowned. "Just don't let your attention wander when we get to Colombia."

Rojas narrowed her eyes. "I was holding my own, naked and unarmed, against three bruiser girls just before you met me. I don't let my mind wander. I *won't* let my mind wander."

"You're no good to me dead, so keep on your toes," Cooper said. He returned to the intel on his smartphone.

She grimaced. Rojas didn't like being told what to do. One of the reasons why she'd become so powerful was that she lived by her own rules. Yet she realized that part of her craved this man's approval.

Cooper was a powerful presence, able to convey praise or condemnation with a simple glance. No man had ever made her feel even a flicker of this kind of…what?

Dependence? No. He actually made her want to step up her game, to prove herself.

Awe? Not quite. Nothing he did seemed magical

to her, not when she saw the truth behind his tactics and his training.

Rojas downed the last of her bourbon, feeling it burn her throat, then closed her eyes, hoping to drift off to less conflicted thoughts.

When the nightmares of blood and mourning came, however, she wasn't disappointed.

RAMON CARRILLO STRUCK a match off the back of his friend Fernando's head. Fernando wasn't his real name; it had been bestowed upon him for his thick neck and broad, bull-like physique. Carrillo didn't even know his real name. Still, it was better than calling him "Toro."

Fernando didn't seem to mind that his scalp was being used to light a match. In fact, Carrillo's gesture made him chuckle.

"How much longer do we have to wait for 'em?" Fernando asked.

Carrillo looked at his watch. "We've got another twenty minutes before the passengers disembark from the plane."

Thanks to bribes, Carrillo, Fernando and a half dozen of their closest friends had managed to avoid metal detectors and security checkpoints at Alfonso Bonilla Aragón International Airport, where Hilde Rojas was supposed to arrive.

Both Carrillo and Fernando, dressed in roomy linen suits, were armed with Brazilian-built knockoffs of Micro Tavor bullpup rifles, 23 inches from nose to butt stock. Thanks to a single point sling, the guns were well-concealed under their loose jackets. When it was time to pull them out, the 5.56 mm NATO rounds would pummel their targets at a rate of seven-hundred to nine-hundred shots per minute.

Hilde Rojas's presence in Cali was either the stupidest idea the United States government had ever had, or it was an intentional sacrifice of a pain in the ass. Sending her back to Medellin might have given her a better chance at survival, but Rojas's enemies were numerous in this city.

The woman had been responsible for the deaths of dozens of Carrillo's friends.

The announcement of her return to Colombia had been practically broadcast over a loudspeaker. She was chum in the water, and Carrillo could see dozens of fellow *tiburons* patrolling the airport, predatory eyes scanning the gates as they waited for their target to show up.

Carrillo and Fernando walked along, anxious and ready for some action. It looked as if three or four different factions were part of this welcoming committee.

Across the room, Carrillo could make out the unmistakable figure of Miguel Villanueva. He was tall and slender, a battered brown Stetson on his head. He carried a small gym bag, which didn't seem out of place.

So, one of the top cops in Colombia was also waiting for Rojas to show up. Maybe more than one.

That would make things stickier. Carrillo and his brethren would have been more than sufficient for a rival gang or airport security, and they would have no problem taking down a lone federal marshal accompanying the former prisoner.

But if Villanueva was here, he might have brought a contingent of Colombian National Police, a platoon or a whole company, even. Sure, Carrillo and his allies were armed as well as any cop would be, but they could easily be outnumbered.

That was when Carrillo spotted *them*. Los Soldados de Cali Nuevos.

Fernando's grimace informed Carrillo that he'd noticed the group, as well.

"Everyone's come out to greet La Brujah," the big bull of a man grumbled. "Should we stick around?"

Carrillo got out his phone as casually as he could. Out of the corner of his eye, he noticed that others were also conferring with their higher-ups.

The Soldados moved in as a vanguard, unmistakable with their military precision and solid formation. Angry eyes regarded each of the other gangs as they swept into the terminal in a flying V, marching apace, not bothering to hide that they were armed.

"Boss," Carrillo said into the phone. "The SNC showed up."

"How many?"

"A dozen," Carrillo responded. "And no one else seems to know what to do."

"Just get out of there," his boss responded. "We do *not* need to get into a shooting war with the Soldiers."

Carrillo assented, then ended the call. All that money spent on obtaining and smuggling the rifles in here, on getting past security. All of it for nothing. He was disappointed that he wouldn't have a chance to shoot down a legend, but considering that even looking the wrong way at a Soldado could inspire a retaliatory massacre, staying wasn't worth the risk.

As they turned and walked away, Carrillo saw people filing off the plane. He paused, scanning those exiting the aircraft.

He was not going to leave without a glimpse of the person they had come here to kill.

Carrillo had photos of Rojas on his phone, which he'd studied extensively, not in small part because of her lean, leggy figure and sultry expression.

But no woman matching Rojas's five-foot-eleven-inch description came through the gate, nor did anyone who appeared to be a federal marshal.

Carrillo watched two men step into the airport. The taller of the two had a gut around him that looked as if he'd seen more time at an all-you-can-eat buffet rather than a gym. His companion was scrawny, his jaw dark with shadow from a day without shaving.

The big man looked right at Carrillo, giving him a once-over.

"Que es esto, gordo?" Carrillo challenged.

The fat guy held up both hands. "No speak-o the Span-o, man!"

"You see something you like?" Carrillo asked him.

Fernando glanced at the big man. "Leave him alone, Ramon," he said tersely.

The fat man winced. "Sorry. Sorry."

Carrillo curled his lip in response to the guy's weakness. The younger man gave his hand a tug, pulling him away.

Carrillo snorted at the tourist and continued following Fernando. His bull-like compatriot steered them toward the washroom, and Carrillo paused just outside.

The big man and his little boyfriend were heading toward him. The fat slob didn't walk too quickly, and he paused, whispering to the scrawny little shit.

"Move along, fatso," Carrillo said.

Before the words were off his tongue, a punch trapped the second half of his insult under his larynx. The Colombian reached up to his windpipe, trying to swallow. In another instant, the fat guy pressed his palm against Carrillo's forehead, ramming his head into the wall. Lights flashed in his field of vision, and before he could get his bearings, he felt himself being dragged into the washroom.

Carrillo heard a door being kicked open, and suddenly he was slammed headfirst into Fernando. A confused, gargling cry filled the air, then Carrillo

felt the toe of a shoe connect with his ear. In the next
heartbeat, there was a violent crunch.

Carrillo blinked, trying to regain his senses as his
head bounced off the side of the stall.

"Jesucristo!" he complained.

A powerful arm slid under his chin and suddenly
he was bent backward.

"Get the rifle off of the other one," a deep, strong
voice said. For a moment, it didn't seem as if it were
the same man who had stepped too close before.…
But how could it not be?

Carrillo's kidney erupted in a blossom of pain as
the man kicked him, then the guy let go and Carrillo
fell unceremoniously on to his back. The fat man
loomed over him, tearing his linen jacket to get to
the Tavor bullpup that hung under one arm, along
with the Argentine Browning Hi-Power in a shoulder
holster and the spare magazine in his pants pocket.

Where was Fernando? Why wasn't he putting up
a fight?

Then the fat man began pulling off his oversized
sweatshirt, showing off the rolls of padding that had
appeared to be a gut. He was wearing a skintight tee
underneath. The man's true torso was lean and powerful, and the arms that had been hidden underneath
the extra-large top were heavily muscled.

"The holster," he ordered.

With little hesitation, Carrillo twisted and writhed
on the floor until he'd managed to get the leather
harness off his back. The stranger inspected him.

"Who are you?" Carrillo asked.

His attacker narrowed his eyes. "The man who thanked you for your guns by allowing you to live. Spread the word. We came here for Los Soldados de Cali Nuevos. If you don't want to die alongside them, stay out of my way."

The skinny guy caught Carrillo's eye, and in a flash, he knew: this was no scrawny American tourist. It was *her.* La Brujah.

Carrillo glanced back at the warrior above him.

"Sit. Stay," the man told him. He shrugged into the oversized shirt again, using it to cover the shoulder holster and the compact rifle on its sling.

With that, the tall stranger and the Witch left the men's room, armed to the teeth.

5

Cooper peered out of the bathroom entrance, then turned back to Rojas. She tugged her hat back over her head, making certain that its bill hung low enough to cover her eyes.

"All set?" he asked her.

"Ready as I'll ever be," Rojas said, patting the weapons beneath her jacket.

She had taken the larger man's M1911 pistol and tucked it into his companion's shoulder holster. Cooper had taken the big guy's holster, the Browning and one of the assault rifles, stripping the other of its ammunition and leaving it lying useless on the bathroom tiles. Rojas liked the M1911 because of its small grip; it fit in her hand perfectly.

As they stepped into the open, Cooper tugged the Browning out, thumbed off the safety and pulled the trigger, aiming at the floor. The noisy report would echo through the terminal, a loud and clear announcement that something was up.

They were out of sight of the SNC and the other thugs, but the sound was unmistakable, and it would bring trouble running.

It was time to split up. As they'd stood in the washroom entrance, they'd made certain that the terminal layout matched the floor plan they'd studied. So far, so good. Cooper ducked into a duty-free shop, while Rojas stood just inside of a newsstand, peering over the racks. Though the gunshot had alarmed everyone around them, no one seemed to suspect that either of them had caused it.

Within moments, the dozen SNC hardmen had caught up to them, and they gathered around the damaged section of floor.

Rojas heard the apparent leader tell the others to spread out. Rojas gave them a casual glance, but kept her poker face, avoiding eye contact or focusing for too long on any of the men. A couple of the Soldados went back toward the washroom.

The bloodied thugs in there would let the New Soldiers know that she and Cooper had breezed past them, presumably in disguise. Still, the gunmen likely wouldn't expect them to linger in the area any longer than necessary, and they'd be focusing on anyone trying to make a quick exit rather than tourists doing some preflight shopping.

When the Soldados returned from the washroom holding up the smaller of the would-be hit men, Rojas gazed up idly, paid for a soft drink and a magazine, and strolled past them.

"...and there's a big bastard, neck broken and nose driven into his skull, sitting on the shitter," she overheard.

The man glanced up, and Rojas fought the urge to spin away, to hide her face. Instead, she calmly turned and headed toward the exit. If he had recognized her in the washroom, there was still a chance that he would hold his tongue about her identity.

A chance. Brunhilde Rojas had not survived this long by trusting the behavior of men sent to kill her. But for the moment, she had to hope the man's terror of the stranger who had spared his life, as well as the strength of her disguise, would be enough.

"You don't see any of your attackers here?" she heard one of the Soldados say behind her.

"No. N-nowhere," the hit man stammered.

"Keep him here," the leader said, his voice radiating with anger. "I'm going to get on the phone."

Rojas knew this was Cooper's moment. For as much as this guy didn't give a damn that he and his armed men were in clear view of the rest of the terminal, he obviously didn't want to be in direct communication with his own commanders where others could eavesdrop.

As Rojas strode farther away from the group around Carrillo, she spotted Cooper slipping into their wake.

THE EXECUTIONER, HAVING DONE his homework on Los Soldados Nuevos de Cali, recognized Rudolpho Arnaz, a mid-level boss in the crime network. Arnaz had grown up on the rough streets of Cali, where he learned to fight and kill as readily as many young men learned to ride a bicycle. According to his rap sheet, by the time Arnaz was in his late teens, he'd murdered four men. Since joining the SNC, after a short stint with the National Police, he'd become a person of interest in dozens of homicides.

Bolan wondered what Arnaz would have thought of Villanueva's presence at the terminal. Bolan trusted the cop, and he was one of the few who was willing to squint and look away when the Executioner came to town. In fact, Villanueva was here to give him and Rojas material support, having deposited a bag full of guns and other assorted gear in an airport locker. Right now, Bolan was good with the Browning Hi-Power, if they could manage to get out of here without a gunfight.

The assembly of hardmen at the terminal was beyond what he could have anticipated. However, most of the civilians had fled, and there were few left to get caught up in any shooting war that might erupt. But for Mack Bolan, even one innocent person caught in the cross fire was one too many.

Bolan zeroed in on Arnaz, who was punching a number into his cell phone. His subordinates stood at a respectful distance, keeping an eye out for Brunhilde Rojas and her escort. Arnaz put the phone to his ear, scanning the terminal for anyone suspicious, but the Executioner had lived his life on the edge of oblivion for so long, he could disappear in plain sight.

Currently, Bolan was pretending to engage in his own call, holding the phone with one hand, clutching the handles of his carry-on with the other. Neck scrunched down, eyes cast on the floor, both hands occupied, he appeared to be in a world all his own. To a casual observer he was just another person on his way to or from a flight. Role camouflage turned him from a finely honed fighting machine to a weary, careless traveler ambling down a corridor.

Arnaz glanced at him, but his gaze didn't linger, so skilled was the illusion that Bolan created. Arnaz headed for an empty row of seats in a waiting area. Bolan followed, plunking himself down a few chairs away from Arnaz, murmuring a one-sided conversation into his phone.

Bolan continued faking his own discussion as he listened in on Arnaz.

"…found evidence that they were here. And they were ready for us to show. No, no, we're not the only crew at the airport. In fact, Rojas and her bodyguard took out one member of another gang and disarmed him and his partner."

There was silence as Arnaz listened to his boss's response.

"Yeah, one guard. And he was in disguise," Arnaz continued. "He was dressed as a fat man. We found the discarded padding on the washroom floor... No, no shots."

Another pause.

"One man kicked to death. The other looks like his face was bounced off every wall in the place. He didn't make a sound, though—the only reason we found the disarmed idiots was because the one who took their firepower put a gunshot into the floor. We came running, then spread out, looking for where he might have gone."

Arnaz was silent for another moment—likely taking orders—then he hung up. That was Bolan's cue.

He stood swiftly, swinging his carry-on around so it smacked Arnaz in the face. The Soldado dropped his cell phone, and before he could recover, Bolan was on top of him. He smashed the heel of his palm into the thug's nose. The blow was at the wrong angle to drive the bridge of the Colombian's nose into his brain, but the impact was still sufficient to daze him. Bolan hooked his other hand around the back of the man's head and dragged it hard into his rising knee. This time, the Executioner felt the nose break, and a spray of crimson splattered the leg of his jeans.

Arnaz flopped back against the bench, and the soldier had a brief instant to carefully aim his next punch. Bolan speared his knuckle into the Colombian's windpipe, crushing it with deadly precision. Arnaz reached up with one hand to clutch at his throat, but there was no chance in hell that he'd be able to force a scream for assistance past his lips.

Bolan cupped the gurgling man's chin with one hand and knotted the fingers of his other hand into Arnaz's hair, tilting his head back.

The ugly crunch of spinal bones grinding against each other was all the confirmation Bolan needed. He set to work searching for the dead man's car keys.

He dialed Rojas. The moment he'd broken off to pursue Arnaz had been her cue to head toward the parking lot.

"Look for a late model Peugeot," he said into the phone.

"There are a couple of them, parked bumper to bumper," Rojas answered. "And there's one guy standing alert and edgy."

"Anyone else with the Soldados' vehicles? Any drivers?" Bolan asked.

"One driver at the ready. No pedestrians in sight."

"I'm on my way. Give me thirty seconds and then open up."

"Thirty seconds," Rojas repeated. "Take the guard, take the driver, dump him and hope he has his keys."

"Arnaz was paranoid enough to keep his keys with him," Bolan told her.

Keys in his pocket, he strode toward the exit.

His timing was perfect. The moment he stepped through the door, he saw Rojas raise the Tavor. The rifle was on single shot, with twenty rounds in the magazine, but at her range, it shouldn't be a problem. From a distance of less than one hundred yards, the high-velocity 5.56 mm rounds would cut through all but the toughest body armor. La Brujah was less than twenty feet from the guard and the driver.

Two sharp cracks preceded the collapse of the Soldado guarding the cars, his face disappearing into a blackish smear of gore as she got him in the side of the head and in the shoulder.

As soon as the guy hit the ground, a car engine roared to life. The driver's reflexes were good, and he threw his vehicle into gear to escape a death trap. Even as he did so, Bolan brought his own stolen Tavor to his shoulder, took aim through the windshield, and milked the trigger. With three quick 5.56 mm rounds to his upper chest, the driver slumped forward, releasing his foot from the accelerator. The car sputtered and stalled.

Rojas rushed to catch up with the stalled car, and Bolan followed. Rojas seemed to have a problem with the door handle, then she sneered and slammed the butt of the bullpup assault rifle into the glass. When the window shattered, she reached in and popped the lock.

Bolan was at the front bumper within moments, pausing only to fire rounds into the grilles of the other three cars left behind. He was sure that no one could start Arnaz's car without the keys, but considering the professional skill sets of the Soldados, he wasn't taking that risk. Damaged engines would slow any pursuit.

"Get the door on my side," Bolan told Rojas. "I'll shoot, you drive."

Rojas pulled out the dead SNC driver, dumping him on to the tarmac. She slipped behind the wheel and opened Bolan's side. "Get in!"

As Rojas pulled out of the parking lot, Bolan exchanged the partially spent magazine from his Tavor with the bathroom guy's fully loaded thirty-rounder. Then he connected Arnaz's cell to his own smartphone.

He hoped that they would be long gone before the remaining SNC thugs could mount a pursuit. The SNC knew that there was someone in Cali, on the hunt for them. They'd been unprepared for Bolan's tactics, and he'd made fools of them, which would only draw more of them into battle.

The gang responsible for the torture and murder of Teresa Blanca had made a date with the Executioner. And now, heads were going to roll.

6

Antonio Carbonez heard the crash of Arnaz's phone as it was knocked from his hand. He listened to the sudden surge of activity on the other end of the line—multiple blows followed by the sickening crack of a breaking neck.

Then the line went dead; Arnaz's killer had ended the call.

But the General of Los Soldados de Cali Nuevos had all the information he needed. The Soldados had been baited with the dangling, juicy worm of Brunhilde Rojas, and in the space of a few moments, the SNC had been compromised. Before he was murdered, Arnaz had told Carbonez that a mysterious stranger, a chameleon who had walked under the noses of his best-trained killers, was actively hunting them.

Logic dictated that Carbonez circle the wagons, fortifying himself against this stranger's incursion…

His phone warbled again. It was Reyes, the driver.

"Sir! The cars are under attack! They killed the—"

Gunfire crackled over the connection, Reyes's headset transmitting the sound of a man releasing his final, ragged breaths. At the same time, the call waiting signal beeped incessantly.

Carbonez didn't need to know whatever his men intended to say. Someone had likely discovered Arnaz, or they were reporting on the sudden gunfire outside the terminal. Carbonez's ire was rising to a boiling point. He squeezed his phone in frustration but continued to listen to the sounds coming from inside Reyes's car.

The clatter of a breaking window. A woman shouting in English.

Something struck Carbonez. There were no alarms going off. The Soldados had forked over sufficient cash to make airport staff and the Cali police look the other way when it came to crossing the security checkpoints with assault rifles. But once things got loud in two locations, the military and the police should have been mobilized and the alarms should have been ringing.

Things were a mess at the airport, but Carbonez hadn't risen to the top of the SNC without the ability to connect seemingly unrelated incidents. Rojas shows up in Colombia, accompanied only by a single man? No obvious police present, except for Inspector Villanueva? Someone had made damned certain that there wouldn't be an honest cop within miles of that terminal, save for Villanueva himself.

Miguel Villanueva was known to have unimpeachable morals, and his mental and physical toughness kept even the hardest cartels at bay. That he showed up in Cali to be in the same vicinity of the arriving Rojas meant that something was cooking. The appearance of that stranger, that shadowy friend of Villanueva, was a signal that blood would be spilled by the gallons. The stranger's most recent appearance had led to a battle on a freighter, leaving corpses and a patina of counterfeit money soaking in the harbor.

Carbonez spent the next few hours stewing as he fielded phone calls from scattered, confused operatives, policemen and journalists whom he had managed to buy off, bribe or threaten into subservience. His tentacles reached far and wide in Cali, throughout Colombia and all the way to Mexico and the United States border.

Carbonez had two options. Go on the defensive and shut down operations for as long as it took this shit storm to blow over, or, put every man on the street, armed to the teeth, and turn Cali upside down in a hunt for this unwelcome guest. The first choice would cause even more damage to the SNC than the loss of lives, in terms of revenue and reputation. The Soldados couldn't afford to be seen as cowards who hid at the first hint of a threat. Carbonez knew the score. Those who had tried sheer force before against Villanueva and his mysterious friend often hadn't lived to tell the tale.

This had to be that spy's fault. Teresa, of the pretty eyes and soft mouth, had managed to worm her way into his office. Then he'd discovered her going through his shit. After a week in the hands of a Zeta interrogation specialist, it came out that she was a US Drug Enforcement Agent.

Carbonez grimaced. He'd heard about a Zetas operation in Texas hit a few days before. He'd wondered if that might have had something to do with the spying Teresa. Even now, that woman was still bedeviling him.

Carbonez rubbed his brow.

"Get the captains on a conference call," Carbonez barked at his secretary. "We're on war footing now. Trouble has come to town."

EVEN WITHOUT OPENING his eyes, Mack Bolan knew that Miguel Villanueva had shown up at the safe house he was sharing with Brunhilde Rojas. The sound of the inspector's car was unmistakable, as was the slam of the car door. One door. This wasn't a group of men disembarking from their shared ride, though Bolan guessed that professionals like the SNC would have parked out of earshot if they were staging an ambush. A kill crew would have hoofed it from a distance rather than give their target any warning.

It had to be Villanueva; he was the only one who knew about the safe house, and they'd dumped the borrowed SNC car miles away. Bolan had also ripped out the dashboard-mounted GPS to prevent tracking, and deactivated the SIMs in both their own phones and the one he'd taken from Arnaz. It was possible the car was still bugged, but they hadn't seen any sign of pursuit since they'd ditched the vehicle, and Bolan doubted the Soldados would have kept their distance once they'd located La Brujah and the dark, deadly stranger by her side.

On foot, Bolan and Rojas were untraceable. Two anonymous humans, making their way through the city.

Once they arrived at the safe house, Bolan changed out of the remnants of his disguise and opted for BDU pants and a short-sleeved shirt with enough room under it to disguise a shoulder holster. He traded the Browning Hi-Power for his preferred sidearms—the Desert Eagle, which he tucked into an inside-the-waistband holster, and his Beretta 9 mm machine pistol, which fit into the shoulder holster.

He was at the front door and opened it before Villanueva could even knock.

"Hola," Bolan greeted the inspector.

"Thanks for not leaving a bunch of bodies at the airport," Villanueva said.

"Was that sarcasm?" Bolan asked, letting the Colombian cop in.

Villanueva shook his head. "I mean bodies of people that count. Not animals like Arnaz or Carrillo."

"I know Arnaz. Which one was Carrillo?" Bolan asked.

"The nobody you left in the washroom. He was from another local gang. Of course, the SNC popped him twice in *la cabeza* after you got away. I guess they shot the messenger," Villanueva said.

Bolan curled his lip. He wasn't too concerned for a would-be assassin's life, but the action of the SNC reinforced their ruthlessness. Carrillo hadn't been a threat, not after being battered and disarmed. The execution of an unarmed man was further proof that he was dealing with barbarian scum.

Bolan waved Villanueva toward a seat.

"Fine. Though I'd hoped that the rest of the Cali thug community would get the word from this Carrillo and stay out of my way," Bolan said. "The more bad guys on the streets, the more chance that a bullet's going to hit a bystander."

"I ordered the clean cops away from the airport," Villanueva assured him. "And all the rotten ones got paid to step off," Villanueva said.

"Not just the cops. Citizens," Bolan corrected.

"I agree. So, you brought in the Brujah?"

Bolan confirmed the question with a bob of his head.

Villanueva swallowed, then tapped his side, where Bolan could make out the shape of a concealed holster. "You're playing a dangerous game."

"When am I not, Miguel? Right now, my gamble is that she has two things more important to her than escape and hurting me. That's protecting her sole remaining kid, and getting revenge against the SNC for killing her older sons."

"This is the woman who personally executed at least one of their fathers," Villanueva warned.

"Then you don't have to join us. Just stay the hell out of our way."

Bolan caught sight of Rojas in the next room. She'd taken off her masculine disguise and was now wearing a snug white tank top and jeans. She'd washed off the stubble makeup and applied some lipstick. Around her hips hung a gun belt, a Glock 19 sitting in the holster.

There was no doubt in Bolan's mind that Rojas was a strong and capable fighter. When he first met her, she'd just survived the attack in the prison showers. Naked and unarmed, she'd managed to hold her own against three larger women. Now, seeing the lean and well-defined muscles the tank top revealed, he had an even sharper impression of La Brujah's strength and power.

He knew it wasn't all physical, though. She'd had iron-fisted control of her operation in New York City, getting personally involved in much of the frequent, brutal violence her cartel inflicted.

All that beauty, all that grace, and yet she still dealt poison, still ordered the deaths of entire families. There was a dark evil inside of her, and Bolan had to remain fully aware that he was dealing with someone who could easily turn on him.

Rojas caught his eye, then smirked.

"Don't worry, I'm not going to bite anyone here."

Villanueva raised his eyebrows but didn't say anything more on the subject. "So what's the rest of your schedule today?" he asked Bolan.

"Waiting for darkness to come."

Rojas stepped out of the bedroom and bared her teeth in joyous malice. "That's right," she said. "Los Soldados better prepare for the witching hour."

7

Guillermo Macco—El Tiburon, to his friends—was surprised that the general put the whole city of Cali on alert. One of the reasons why he'd thrown in his lot with the SNC was because of its elite standing. Los Soldados wouldn't be intimidated or pushed into a panic.

But that was before the rumors that La Brujah was coming to town. Brunhilde Rojas had mentored under Medellin's last big boss before that man died in a blaze of glory and gunfire. She was heir to a throne of blood and thunder, and if the US government had sent her back to Colombia, they were either looking to kill her, or to drop a live grenade amongst the Cali cartels.

And from the way Carbonez was talking, the grenade theory didn't seem so far from the truth. So far, three Soldados were cooling meat on a slab, and the cops from every precinct had developed a sudden urge to take vacation time—even the honest ones.

With Carbonez on the paranoid path and the cops taking to the sidelines, Macco was fully aware how serious the situation was. But that was all right. He hadn't earned the name El Tiburon because he loved eating fish. He'd worked his way into the SNC with his own dangerous, deadly skills. He took bites out of his competition—literally—and he was a savage predator who'd stalked Cali for long enough to build a reputation and merit a good ranking in the SNC.

Macco heard from Carbonez that another man was in town, working arm in arm with the Colombian Witch.

Macco had placed armed men at all the doors of the tenement, and more than a few of them had taken a snort of nose candy in order to maintain their "edge." Macco wasn't normally one to have his people use the product, but a small hit was just the thing to sharpen their focus and keep them alert.

So what if La Brujah and her little friend were in town?

He was the Shark, dammit! Macco was the apex predator in this part of Cali.

And to enforce that, Macco had his "teeth" ready. The weapon had taken years of cobbling and refinement, but now it was one of the most devastating guns on Cali's streets. It was a standard RPK light machine gun, but with many of its parts changed

over to make it handier, quicker to use in combat.
Its 23.2-inch barrel had been replaced with an 8-inch
front end, enabling Macco to move swiftly through
tight doorways. He'd also put a fore grip on it, along
with a laser pointer which allowed him to shoot from
his hip. He wore a sling, which helped balance the
heavy laser, drum and stabilizing weights he'd put
into the forward grip to control recoil. On full auto,
the gun produced a fireball the size of a soccer ball
that could cut a man in half, five 7.62 x 39 mm
rounds tearing into a human torso in less than a
second.

Macco had the weapon resting on his desk, a
live round in the chamber, and another seventy-five
ready. More drums were clipped to his load-bear-
ing vest; he and the rest of his crew were all in full
military gear, as per SNC standard combat protocol.
Backing up his deadly little chainsaw-like submachine gun was a brace of .357 Magnum revolvers.
Macco was ready for war.

It was getting dark outside, and there seemed to
be a pall over the whole city. What had earlier been
a bustling, active neighborhood where Macco's boys
could sling coke with impunity was now barren and
quiet. Street lamps burned orange, and it was eerily
silent. Usually, Macco didn't mind the heat and humidity, but tonight it was absolutely stifling, smothering him.

Maybe La Brujah really did have some kind

of magic power; perhaps she was controlling the weather, making things thicker, mustier. Or maybe his nerves were so on edge that he was willing to believe anything.

Gullibility was one thing that he couldn't afford right now, not when there was a storm coming to town. Weather didn't bend itself to the will of any woman, especially not some bitch who'd managed to get herself thrown in prison seven years ago.

The other man, well…his presence had probably just been hyped by rumors. The guy had been talked up enough to get Carbonez all wired up, and if the general was nervous…

Shit rolls downhill, Macco thought. El Tiburon didn't feel too much need to worry. He had an army of twenty guys ready to throw down on any fool who tried to step up to them.

A strange *pop* sounded in the office, and suddenly, Macco's desk lamp went out. For a moment, he thought it might have just been the bulb, but then the ceiling fan slowed. He scooped his RPK off of the desk, throwing the strap over one shoulder for support.

He turned the laser on and flicked the switch on the gun's mounted flashlight, a big blazing halogen unit running off two big D-cell batteries. It would light his way and blind anyone in his path.

"Nice try!" Macco shouted. "But this is the twenty-first century. We have flashlights!"

A moment later, Macco's window shattered, and

something slammed into his RPK. The halogen light hit the floor, plunging the office into darkness once more.

Macco tried to recover control of the rifle, but a massive impact struck his body, sending him spinning. He bounced off the top of his desk and spiraled into the wall, bashing his head on the windowsill. He reached out to catch his balance, but both palms landed on jagged splinters of glass.

"Fuck! Fuck!" Macco shouted. He withdrew his bleeding hands and lost his footing. His face met with the same shards that had torn his palms to ribbons. Macco struggled to crawl across the floor despite the agony of his butchered hands and the blood flowing into his eyes. Thumps of suppressed gunfire filled the air. Macco's shoulder bumped the side of his desk, and he inched along until he could get beneath it for cover. As soon as he was underneath, he rolled on to his back, plucking at the splinters with trembling fingers.

A body crashed to the rug next to him, and Macco let out a yelp of surprise. He turned and saw one of his best gunmen lying on the carpet. Well, most of him. There was a cavernous hole where the top of his head should have been. Even louder gunfire rippled up from downstairs. Someone was going to town with a non-silenced weapon. On this floor, windows shattered in the other rooms along the corridor. "Stop it!" Macco yelled, catching sight of his gunman's

ruined face once more. "Just stop it," he murmured.
"I'm the goddamned Shark…"

THE PLAN WAS FOR Rojas to man the sniper rifle while
Bolan went inside the tenement. Rojas was in position, using an M4 rifle with a 300 AAC Blackout
and a suppressor baffle. The gunshots wouldn't be
audible or bright enough for the men in the building
to see them coming, or home in on Rojas herself.

"How's it going?" Bolan asked over his hands-
free radio.

"This is fun," Rojas answered with grim satisfac-
tion in her tone. There was a true note of enjoyment,
too, but mostly she seemed relieved. Each pull of the
trigger allowed her to vent anger and grief over the
callous, cowardly murders of her sons.

Bolan allowed her that.

He was also carrying an M4, but his was loaded
with .30 caliber rounds that produced minimal muzzle flash. Sure, the blasts were loud and bright, but
they wouldn't be blinding or deafening.

Bolan expected the SNC gunmen in the tenement
to be on full alert. Stealing a glance through a first-
floor window, he saw that they seemed jittery, on
edge. They *were* alert, but they were clearly so over-
stimulated—possibly on coke—that the first sign of
danger was all it took to unleash chaos. Bolan simply
tossed an empty can through the front doorway and
three of the Soldados opened fire. One of them took
out another, leaving only two guards in the foyer.

The stubby M4 growled, ripping through muscle and ribs, shredding lungs and hearts with brutal efficiency. Within an instant, there were three dead thugs in the room. Bolan leaped into the hallway to see men reacting frantically to Rojas's window-shattering shots.Bolan charged down the hall, greeting every challenge with a snarl of bullets, blasting craters into the torsos of El Tiburon's fighters. Some of them wore body armor, but the M4's deadly sputter struck with enough force to slow them down, allowing Bolan to adjust aim and put bullets into their exposed heads and throats.

The Executioner surged across the ground floor, his senses fine-tuned to everything around him. Between Rojas's sniping, Bolan's blitz and the gunmen's agitated state, the SNC didn't stand a chance in this tenement.

It took all of a minute and two thirty-round magazines to completely clear the first story. The second story was alive with breaking glass and screams of terror and pain. Rojas wasn't allowing the Soldados a moment of respite.

Bolan had supplied the woman with low-light and magnification optics which could squeeze every ounce of accuracy out of the rifle, and from the sounds of it, she was taking advantage of her concealed position.

She'd obviously done a lot of long-range shooting, even though the distance wasn't great. At most, her shots would have to travel forty yards, but even so, her accuracy and the sheer amount of destruction she was wreaking on the tenement were impressive. By the time Bolan reached the second floor corridor, only a few men remained within sight. They were cowering in a corner, seeking protection against the drywall.

The Executioner shouldered his rifle and drilled one of the men through the side of his head with a single round. The other Soldado let out a scream as he saw his friend's head go to pieces, and waved his machine pistol wildly. In the dark hallway, Bolan was a wraith among the shadows.

Bolan ripped the terrified gunman open with a tri-burst from his compact rifle, eliminating that threat before continuing across the floor.

"On two," Bolan told Rojas. "Don't shoot me."

"Wouldn't dream of it," La Brujah replied. "I'm saving all my ammo and hatred for the enemy."

Bolan checked each small apartment, sweeping doorways with cautious efficiency in case there were gunmen inside. Alert and in the moment, he moved onward, keeping close to the interior wall to protect himself against a potential ambush. The drywall between the hall and the residences wouldn't stop a bullet, especially not at close range, but if he wasn't seen, he wouldn't provoke a shot through the flimsy barrier between himself and the enemy.

Easy, certain steps carried him to the end of the hallway, and sure enough, all he found were the dead

Soldados that Rojas had taken out of the game. One floor left.

He crept back to the stairwell, pausing at each doorway in case someone had been playing possum on his first pass.

That precaution saved Bolan's life. A wounded gunman in an otherwise empty foyer struggled to his knees, bracing himself with one hand and gripping a pistol with the other. With a lightning-fast reflex, the Executioner riddled the Colombian with a burst of auto fire.

That was the last of any opposition on the floor, and all Bolan heard as he climbed the next flight of stairs was a lone grunt of pain and effort. The sound told the Executioner that he was dealing with someone who was still striving to stay alive and keep going.

"Anyone else on the top floor?" Bolan asked Rojas.

"No movement. They're either hiding from the slugs I put through the windows, or dead," she replied. "I left Macco…able to communicate."

"I hear him. Keep an eye out for anyone else showing up to this party."

It wasn't just a cursory warning. Los Soldados de Cali Nuevos were ruthless, and sacrificing one of their own officers and his men was not beyond them. Sending out advance scouts was one way that commanders could make certain that the route they were taking wasn't lined with ambushes. It meant sacrificing the men sent on ahead, but for the greater good of the force, an officer could accept the losses.

Still, it was highly unlikely that General Carbonez would have had the prescience to pick the exact commander the Executioner would go after. All of the SNC's forces in the city were targets. Macco was just important enough to send a message, but he wouldn't have been an obvious first hit in Rojas's revenge sweep.

Bolan scanned each room as he had on the lower levels until he reached Macco's office, making certain no one was lying in ambush. He swung into the room, taking in the grisly mess Rojas had made of the cocaine commando. One eye had a shard of glass sticking out of it, and he was bleeding from his hands and face. Macco wore an armored vest, but it had been torn, a breast pouch smashed by La Brujah's shot.

A mangled light machine gun with a stubby barrel hung off the man's shoulder, but Macco seemed to have forgotten it was there. "No...no...no..." Macco swayed side to side beneath his desk. El Tiburon, once the top of the food chain in this neighborhood, had been reduced to no more than a nervous flounder.

"*Si,*" Bolan said.

Macco looked up, his good eye wide with shock.

Bolan let his carbine dangle in its sling. "Your phone."

Macco glanced around. He'd lost a lot of blood,

so he seemed almost drunk, no longer with it. "On the desk...don't..."

Bolan spotted the cell phone at the edge of the desk. He grabbed it and pulled up the recent calls screen. There was an unlisted number, likely a call from Carbonez on a burner phone. He hit the dial-back and waited.

"You gonna kill me?" Macco whimpered.

Bolan put his index finger to his lips, shushing the dazed Macco. The number had been disconnected, so Bolan hung up. "How do you get in contact with your general?"

"Contacts...under floater," Macco said. He held out a shredded hand in front of his face. "How'd my hands get so messed up?"

"Your window broke. I think you tried cleaning it up," Bolan said gently, in an effort to keep the dazed, bleeding man calm as he found the entry in the SNC lieutenant's phone.

"Macco? What is it?" said the voice on the line. "Did you make contact?"

"He did," Bolan said, his tone icy. "Right now, he doesn't look like he'll be much use to anyone."

There was silence on the other end.

"What's wrong, General?" Bolan pressed.

"Nothing your death wouldn't fix," Carbonez said after clearing his throat.

"Your boys tried their best, but they're only pretenders to the throne."

"Boss! I can't see out of one of my eyes!" Macco shouted. "What's wrong with me?"

"Shut that son of a bitch up," the SNC commander snarled.

"Fine," Bolan returned. He pulled his Beretta and fired twice, the sharp crack of the pistol resounding in the room. He would have bled out, and it was likely that the glass had punctured the thin bone at the back of the socket, affecting Macco's brain. He was already a dead man; the Executioner had just cut his suffering short.

"That's one group down," Bolan told Carbonez. "Tell your boys not to use coke to keep their edges sharp. Not that it matters for Macco and his school of dead fish."

"Why are you doing this?" Carbonez asked.

"Teresa. The girl you sent to be tortured and killed," Bolan answered.

"What? You were in love with her or something?"

"No. I didn't even know her. But I saw what you asked the Zetas to do for you. So I'm going to take you and your whole army apart so you can't do that to anyone else. By the time I'm finished, you'll be begging for a bullet in the head."

With that, Bolan shut off the phone. He looked down at Macco. He could tell that the poor bastard had done most of this damage to himself, that it hadn't been Rojas's shots, exactly, that had left him in this state. But it was still a gruesome scene.

This was just a little evidence of the hatred Brunhilde Rojas was harboring for those who had killed her sons. Her quest for vengeance would likely make death seem preferable to anyone who tried to get in her way.

Bolan would ride this tiger for now. He had experience with lethal, potentially traitorous allies.

Right now, he knew he'd picked the right weapon for the job. He just hoped it wouldn't explode in his face.

8

Carbonez grumbled as the phone went dead. "You want me to beg for a bullet in the head? You want me to beg?"

He hurled the device across the room, and it shattered against the wall. The commotion and his accompanying roar brought a couple of his bodyguards racing through the door, rifles out and ready. Carbonez glared at them. Standing unarmed, in front of his desk, seething with rage, he made the two gunmen lower their weapons and back out slowly, eyes wide at the sight of him.

Carbonez was not a small man, but he wasn't a tall stack of muscle, either. He was wiry, just under five foot ten, but his body was hard as steel. His clenched fists and the blaze of hatred in his eyes was enough to cow even the hardiest of soldiers.

"Lo siento," the bodyguard whispered.

"Leave me be." Carbonez stuffed his fiery temper back down into his gut. His tone cooled, and he felt the blood pressure ebb from his cheeks and the veins on his forehead.

"We've got word that someone hit El Tiburon's..."

"Yes. That's who I just got off the phone with," Carbonez told the bodyguard. "Not Macco, but the bastard who killed him."

"El Tiburon is...dead?" the guard asked.

Carbonez nodded. "Get on the troops. This is worse than we anticipated."

The guard's eyes widened, and then he turned, taking off. The other man stayed at his post but allowed the office door to close.

Carbonez leaned against the desk with one hand, brushing his hair back into place after his fit of rage. He'd allowed this man—this *American*—to get on his nerves with those petty threats. Even so, he resented losing his temper. Carbonez, after all of his years as a JUNGLA commando, prided himself on professionalism. As former members of the JUNGLA, an anti-narcotics arm of Colombia's national police force, he and the rest of the SNC founders were highly trained special operations troopers. He'd worked side by side with the American Drug Enforcement Agency, and had received training from the US Special Forces, aka the Green Berets.

His was a lineage of warriors with impeccable skill and discipline. Losing his shit like that was something he'd thought that he'd left behind long ago. And yet, after the debacle at the airport and the death of El Tiburon and his whole team, Carbonez's old temperament issues seemed to be resurfacing. He wished he hadn't displayed that tiny weakness to his two guards.

When he lost his cool, he showed those two men that he was less than the cold-blooded, highly capable commander who would carry them through countless battles. Gaining control over Cali and developing a booming trade was one thing. He'd fended off other cartels trying to regain lost ground, and so far, the Soldados were still ruling the roost. This was the first serious challenge they'd faced, and he couldn't have his men doubting his leadership.

"Keep your cool," Carbonez told himself.

He strode over to his chair and plopped down into it.

He pulled out a replacement burner. With a few taps on his computer, he set up the network so that his soldiers could connect with the new phone—everyone except Macco.

That man, La Brujah's "friend," had killed Macco, quickly and cleanly.

And he'd promised that Carbonez would be begging for that same, sweet release.

The general grimaced at that concept. People were supposed to beg *him* for that mercy.

He ran his thumb along the armrest, feeling the knife he kept under there at all times. His office was festooned with hidden weapons; in fact, the entire

SNC headquarters had similar caches. He'd prepared for all manner of crises.

He suspected this American was some kind of vigilante, or someone hired by a rival cartel to bring the SNC down without opening themselves up to assault.

The SNC had dealt with pretenders to the throne before, and they'd torn apart those vigilante sock puppets. Carbonez wondered who could have sent La Brujah and her American friend to challenge him.

If he figured that out, he could easily turn the tables on them. He was sure of it.

Someone was trying to play Carbonez, but that was their last, fatal mistake.

BRUNHILDE ROJAS RELISHED the role she'd returned to Cali to play. Cooper had told her she was essentially bait for the SNC, but she didn't mind. People were paying attention to her now, and Cali was a hotbed of rumor and excitement; the Witch had returned, and she was bringing hell with her. It was the same rush she'd felt when she'd reigned in New York.

It was nearing dawn, and tourists and shift workers were coming in from a night of activities. Most of the decent people on the main thoroughfares were oblivious to the war being waged in Cali right now. With her black skirt, her knee-high boots and red, form-hugging silk blouse, Rojas blended in with the people heading home from the clubs. She had a maroon clutch purse in faux crocodile hide, inside of which was her weapon.

La Brujah carried an FN Five-seveN pistol. The 5.7 mm round that the handgun was named after was capable of punching through Kevlar helmets and flak jackets at close ranges. With a twenty-round magazine in place and an extra one tucked in a garter under her skirt, she was more than capable of fighting off a small army.

She herself was wearing throat-to-crotch Kevlar beneath her clubbing clothes, complete with trauma plates. Armored as she was, Rojas was still vulnerable, particularly in the face and neck regions. Her shoulders, wrists and legs were also bare. But Rojas had the advantage of knowing the tactics of the drive-by assassins she was watching out for. It would be two men, one small, agile motorbike. The second rider would be packing a fully automatic weapon. Both men would be clad in full helmets and body armor under racing leathers.

The motorcycle would pull up on a target and open fire before zooming off. The driver would duck through an alley or circumvent a traffic jam. If the target was in motion on the highway, the bike would still be able to catch up and riddle the passengers with bullets. Despite the din of the late-night crowds, Rojas had her ears pricked for the whine of a bike motor. Somewhere on the streets, Cooper was shadowing her, but she saw no sign of him.

"When you say shadow, you mean it," she said into her hands-free radio.

"You're looking a little paranoid there," Cooper responded.

Rojas smirked. So he was nearby. Watching and listening.

"Hilde Rojas wouldn't be on the streets of Cali without being aware of her surroundings," she shot back. "And don't worry, I can't detect a single hair's worth of your presence."

"What matters to me is the rest of the folks looking for us," Cooper said. "I've got movement."

Rojas glanced over her shoulder, and sure enough, a block away a single headlight blazed in the predawn gloom. The unmistakable snarl of the engine reached her ears, and as it approached, she made out the two helmeted figures riding it. She popped the clasp on the clutch casually, readying herself to pull out the Five-SeveN when the moment came.

The crowd had thinned around her. Even the most dense and inebriated carousers understood that a dirt bike on a city street meant bad news, especially in Cali. Rojas stood boldly in the open, another sign that there was trouble afoot. Her red lips turned up in a smile, dark eyes unblinking as the would-be assassins drew closer.

"Them?" she whispered.

"Gun," Cooper confirmed.

She gripped her pistol, letting the clutch fall to the ground as she brought the Five-SeveN to eye level. The muzzle flashed brilliantly, producing a fireball and a harsh crack. She'd aimed a few feet ahead of the motorcycle driver's helmet, and as the gun jumped with the slight recoil, the bike swerved violently. The tinted visor of the rider's helmet disappeared, shattering as a bullet punched through it. Once the slug hit the man's skull, he lost all control of his vehicle.

The gunman on the back triggered his own weapon, but with the bike careening in the street, his burst of automatic fire sizzled skyward before both men caught a case of road rash, skidding on the pavement with the motorcycle pulling them along.

Rojas sighted the two fallen assassins, then tapped off high-velocity bullets as quickly as she could. La Brujah was nothing if not precise when it came to shooting, and by the time the killers and their motorcycle ground to a halt, the driver was most certainly dead, the other man wounded and struggling to get out from under the weight of the vehicle.

Rojas strode off of the curb, glad she wasn't wearing stiletto heels as she charged toward the downed gunner. He still had his weapon in hand, a stubby little machine pistol, but Rojas took aim as she walked, pumping three bullets into the shooter's chest.

In moments, the motorcycle assassination crew was finished, and Rojas lowered the gun, sweeping the safety on. She looked back to see where she'd dropped her clutch as another warning growled in her ear.

"Cover!" Cooper ordered.

Two more bikes swung on to the street. The first pair of bikers must have been keeping in touch with their colleagues.

Rojas found the solid protection of a stone planter in front of a hotel, ducking behind it as automatic weapons fired hot streams of death toward her.

Another type of gunshot mixed in with the sound of the machine pistols. It was a dull drumbeat in the middle of the staccato rat-a-tat-tat, followed immediately by human yelps and the screech of metal as the bikes were hit.

Safe behind the planter, Rojas reached down and pulled the spare Five-SeveN magazine from her thigh strap, feeding it into the handgun. She hoped it would be enough.

She peered cautiously at the street and saw the skidding motorcycles smash into each other, throwing the riders off their backs. She heard more dull gunshots and saw blood begin to pool beneath the fallen thugs. Thanks to Cooper, none of these men would be getting back up.

"Fall back to rendezvous B," Cooper said over the hands-free device. "We're drawing attention further up the road."

Rojas obeyed, pushing to her feet and racing up the driveway beside the hotel. Behind it, she turned into a back alley, then continued on. How she got to the second meet-up spot was just a matter of details, but she wasn't going to take a straight line. Pausing at a dumpster, she found a paper bag and jammed the handgun into it. The bag didn't match her outfit, but it was better than racing through the streets with a huge pistol in her hand.

As she continued on her route, she wondered at the nature of the "attention" Cooper had mentioned, and why he'd asked her to retreat.

Whatever it was, Rojas couldn't help but feel a pang of concern for the big American.

FORTUNATELY, THE CROWDS had dispersed when the first shots had been fired, and from his vantage on the second floor of an aboveground parking garage, Bolan could see that this stretch of city street was now empty.

Except, of course, for the two SUVs rushing up the boulevard. These had to be more Soldados. The headlights were off, and the vehicles approached like shadows in the half light.

Bolan shouldered his rifle; he was still making use of the M4 with .300 Blackout cartridges. The black trucks were big enough targets that he could afford to switch to full-auto.

Bolan opened up, sending a stream of slugs crashing into one windshield. The heavyweight sniper rounds turned the tinted windscreen into a spider web of cracked glass. The SUV swerved under the assault, but the driver showed good reflexes. He pulled a skid, yanking the parking brake on and letting the big ride slide sideways on its tires, bringing it to a halt.

The other truck came to a more controlled stop, but the Executioner rained down a burst into its hood. Fifteen rounds tore through the black sheet metal, and within a moment, smoke wisped out of the grille. Bolan dumped the spent magazine and fed it another.

There was no way he would allow two death squads to remain on the streets of Cali. The more Soldados he took out down here, the fewer he'd have to deal with later on.

Riflemen spilled out of the first vehicle, brandishing M4 carbines. Being former JUNGLA commandos, the Soldados were packing Colombian military hardware and the same jungle fighting gear that they'd been trained with during their time in joint DEA and Special Forces operations.

Though Bolan had been well-concealed in the garage, the muzzle flash of his M4 had given the thugs a clue to his location. The Soldados' auto fire hammered at the concrete rail a few feet to his right.

Bolan made his way around a pillar and had a better angle on the shooters who were using their well-armored truck for cover. The Executioner disabused them of their illusion of safety with a suppressed growl from his Beretta, blowing the brains out of one of the Cali soldiers.

The Beretta had a much lower profile than the rifle, so for a few moments, his opponents didn't know where the attack was coming from. They seemed to be trying to sight a second sniper, not expecting the same man to switch weapons mid-battle. Bolan punched out two more tri-bursts, downing a pair of Soldados before someone spotted his shadow next to a support pillar.

Bullets zipped by Bolan's position, but he had plenty of concrete to shield him. However, several men were now making for the entrance of the garage.

The Soldados would be coming at him in close quarters, which didn't bother Bolan in the least. The more contained the combat, the less likely that civilians could get caught in the cross fire. But he still had to deal with the men who remained by their SUVs. He pulled a hand grenade from his battle harness and lobbed it out of the garage. It bounced twice and came to a rest underneath the first SUV he'd fired on.

The gruesome crack of explosives filled the air, and the truck flipped over. Shrapnel tore at the ankles of the gunmen using the vehicle as cover, and the driver was still inside. Flames licked off the undercarriage of the shattered vehicle, growing closer to the fuel tank. A secondary explosion shook the truck, crumpling it like a pop can.

The blast caused a couple of the men heading for the garage to pause, looking back at the column of fire and devastation. Shocked and dismayed, they were flat-footed and easy targets for the Executioner. The two Soldados fell to the ground with a single .300 Blackout bullet in each of their skulls.

That left four more men rushing into the parking garage for Bolan to deal with.

So far, so good.

9

Hector Delapaz paused as he watched two of his brethren fall, cored through the head with a rifle bullet in the wake of the erupting van. Though he had his combat rifle in hand, he suddenly felt very small and vulnerable. The three other SNC commandos with him were equally hesitant to bring this battle ever closer to the man who had killed so many of their own. Six men on bikes, a half dozen from the SUVs.

Delapaz swallowed. "We don't cower. We attack. By the numbers. Cover each other. We're heavily armed, well-equipped and trained professionals."

The other three men seemed doubtful, gazing warily into the shadows of the parking lot. Who knew what kind of opposing force they could run into in there? Delapaz slapped the closest of his comrades. "We outnumber them. Keep cool and follow your training."

Delapaz began to turn away from the carnage in the middle of the avenue, but a dark shape suddenly dropped down in front of him. Startled but in control, Delapaz brought up his automatic rifle before his brain had even made sense of the sudden apparition.

A hand with a grip of steel clutched the barrel of Delapaz's weapon, wrenching it from his sweaty palms. He felt a tug on his shoulder sling, and he lost his balance. A bright flash of light and pain lanced through his head. Then everything went black.

HAVING STUNNED THE leader of the group, Mack Bolan lunged forward and shoved the limp figure into the man closest to them. The dazed commando had been the only one who'd caught the flicker of movement as Bolan rappelled over the railing and dropped to street level, almost literally landing on top of the Soldados.

The second gunman staggered, letting out a cry of dismay at Delapaz's clumsiness. The shout further distracted the other two, giving the Executioner his chance. He snagged the handle on the back of one Colombian's fighting vest. The D-ring was meant for dragging a wounded soldier to safety and medical assistance. The Executioner had another purpose in mind. He wrenched the Cali commando backward and drove his knee into the man's spine.

The thug shouted in agony, releasing the carbine

in his hands to clutch at his back. Another Soldado struck out at Bolan, but he rammed his elbow into the side of that man's neck, a powerful blow that dropped the thug to the parking garage floor.

The leader was still dazed, but the last man standing had now gotten his bearings and aimed his rifle at Bolan. The Executioner pinned the carbine against his opponent's chest, taking the gun out of this equation. With his other hand, he clawed at the Colombian's eyes. The man screamed in pain, bringing his hands up to his face.

Bolan snatched both of his wrists, getting leverage on his enemy. With a twist, he hurled the stunned opponent across his hip, slamming him head-first into the concrete. To make certain he was down for the count, the Executioner kicked him in the temple, rendering him unconscious.

The man he'd kneed in the back caught Bolan's attention. He was busy trying to stand. Once more, Bolan yanked the D-ring on the guy's vest, pulling up hard, then smashing his face into the ground. A geyser of blood gushed from his nostrils, and before he could even reach up to stanch the flow, Bolan gave him a karate chop where his neck met his shoulder.

Nerves short-circuited from the impact, and the man crumpled into a senseless heap at the warrior's feet.

He turned back to the leader and gave him a quick slap to bring him back around.

"Whuh…"

"Call Carbonez," Bolan ordered.

"We don't…"

Bolan gave him a light tap on the cheek. "Call the next person up the food chain from you, then."

The man's eyes widened as he took in his surroundings and Bolan's intimidating presence. He felt around his vest pocket for his phone as Bolan stripped him of magazines and the other gear in his vest. When he found the guy's knife, Bolan pressed the button and the blade sprang into place.

"Don't stab me," the man pleaded.

Bolan fixed him with a hard stare. "I don't see you calling your supervisor."

The leader blinked, then looked at his phone, connecting with his lieutenant.

"B-boss?"

Bolan grabbed the phone from the commando's hand.

"What's going on?" the voice on the phone asked. "I'm not getting anything from anyone at the scene…"

"Sorry to say that all but four of your men are dead," Bolan said. "We hung La Brujah out as bait, and you morons fell for it."

"The other…guys…alive?" the fellow on the ground asked.

"Not that it'll help you," Bolan told the stunned gunman. "Your bosses might not let you live for blowing this hit. Now you, boss," he continued.

"Screw you!" The phone disconnected.

Using his own PDA, Bolan sent the data from the call to Stony Man so they could zero in on this commander's location. Then he hit redial on the Soldado's phone, and the same man picked up. He was ranting in Spanish almost faster than Bolan could translate, but that didn't matter. Bolan just needed him to stay on the line so the tech crew in the Blue Ridge Mountains could do their work.

Bolan's PDA buzzed, and he watched as a map of Cali zoomed in on the officer's location. Within a few moments, he had an address and a name.

"Manuel," Bolan said, cutting the man off mid-rant.

"Oh, no," the officer muttered.

"I'm coming by to pay you a visit."

"Coming?" Manuel Herrera asked.

"See you soon," Bolan said, hanging up.

The dazed man blinked again. Bolan knocked him out with a kick that shattered his jaw.

It was time to meet up with Rojas.

HILDE ROJAS PEELED out of the body armor. The exertion of rushing to the rendezvous with Cooper, especially in Cali's early morning humidity, had left her hot and sticky. Now that they were back at the safe house, she was glad to be free of the heavy protective vest.

She reached for cargo pants and a long-sleeved compression shirt, her take on the blacksuit. They only planned to stop here briefly, changing gear and loading up on ammo.

They'd already taught Los Soldados Nuevos de Cali to be afraid of the dark. Now it was time to show them the daylight hours were no time for a siesta.

"So, Manuel Herrera, eh?" Rojas called to Cooper as she slipped into her fighting clothes. "When I was last in Medellin, I heard he was an up-and-comer here in Cali. He was taking out honest cops and reporters off of the back of a motorcycle."

"I had one of our ambushers call his boss. It looks like Herrera earned himself a promotion in the business," Cooper replied.

Rojas stepped out of the bedroom as Cooper strapped on his gun belt, complete with the massive .44 Magnum Desert Eagle, hung low, belted into place around his thigh. His Beretta 9 mm was in its shoulder holster.

Cooper covered the holster and the short-sleeved compression top he wore with a long, loose Hawaiian shirt that concealed the massive gun in its fast-draw rig on his hip. Still, even a small bump on the sidewalk would reveal the firepower beneath the warrior's clothes.

That told Rojas that they were going by car.

"What is the plan for Herrera's place?" she asked.

"You get to see how well you do with a grenade launcher off of the practice range," Cooper answered.

With that, he opened the safe house door and stepped outside.

Before following him, Rojas did something she hadn't thought of doing since she was ten years old.

She made a sign of the cross and whispered a prayer for help.

10

"How the hell did you manage to blow a hit on one woman?" Carbonez sneered into the phone. "I mean, sure, I can see one motorcycle team failing. I can even understand two, but by all reports, there shouldn't be two of my Land Rovers burnt to useless husks in the street."

Herrera felt fire swell in his chest in response to the general's derision.

"If you look at those reports—" He bit off his words, remembering that Carbonez was not the kind of man who tolerated back talk. "Sorry, sir."

"Fourteen more of our fellow soldiers are on their way to the morgue," Carbonez said. "And a little punk like you is going to start raising your voice?"

"I am sorry, sir. Delapaz said that there was a sniper in a parking garage. He ambushed the other teams. And he was armed with some heavy fire-power."

"Yet, with all of that firepower, he left four of your men alive," Carbonez countered. "Tell me why I shouldn't take that as a hint that you're colluding with these bastards?"

"He was sending a message. To me…and then on to you."

"The message being what?" Carbonez asked.

Herrera hesitated. "Your phone network…he said he was coming for a visit."

There was a cold silence on the other end, and the captain almost wished Carbonez would roar or curse, if only to break the tension. Instead, when Carbonez spoke again, the steady calm in his voice made Herrera's blood run cold.

"So he's got a location on us. He must have hacked into the SNC's network or something?"

"Yes, sir," Herrera replied. He closed his eyes, wincing as he braced for the oncoming storm.

"And you thought to bury the lede of this story for *how* long into this conversation?" Carbonez asked.

Herrera swallowed. "I don't know how long this conversation has been going on. And I have not had much of an opportunity…"

"The American could be on his way to you. Hell, he could be standing on your front steps right now. And you decide it's a good time to shoot the shit?"

"Sir…"

"If you interrupt me again, pull your pistol out,

shove it in your mouth and suck it until the clip is empty," Carbonez snarled.

Herrera went silent, feeling the blood drain from his face.

He could hear the general pacing back and forth, burning off the ire sizzling under the surface.

When the general spoke again, his voice was more controlled. "Based on the attack at Macco's, we know this bastard strikes at night. Skulking around in the dark, like a coward. You should have a few hours, Herrera. You'd better not let me down again."

Herrera swallowed. The livery garage where he headquartered was already revving up for full alert. When the cold-voiced killer who'd wiped out the assassination squads warned of an inevitable meeting, he'd pulled in his remaining hunters. Even though it was hours until sunset—the American and La Brujah's next window of opportunity—he intended to be fully prepared well before then. Herrera couldn't afford any margin of error.

Thankfully, with two more armored vehicles on the premises, they'd have a chance to deal with these two interlopers.

Once Carbonez was finished chewing him out, Herrera would head right back to work, organizing the troops, making sure everyone was primed and ready for the impending assault.

Suddenly, the ground heaved beneath him, and a deafening roar swept through his office. The next thing he knew, he was on his hands and knees, ears ringing. Books and files had been thrown from shelves and framed pictures had been knocked off of their hooks on the walls.

"The fuck was that?" Carbonez shouted into the phone.

"We're under attack!" Herrera snapped back in response. "I thought he would only attack us at night!"

Herrera scrambled to his desk and pulled open the top drawer. He plucked out his handgun and jammed it into his waistband. If the American and the Witch were attacking in the bright light of day, then the general wasn't so damned worthy of Herrera's respect. The moron had lied to him, and because of that, he could already smell the reek of burned flesh on the other side of his office door.

"More of my men are dying out there! And *you* are the one who these bastards are targeting!" Herrera continued. "You'd better pray to whatever god you believe in that they fucking kill me, because if they don't, I'm coming for your ass!"

Herrera couldn't tell if the phone was still working or if Carbonez had hung up, but he didn't care.

"I will take your operation apart piece by piece, until you're begging me to kill you," he said before hanging up himself.

Another hammering fist of high explosives made the walls shudder, and Herrera stumbled through the half-opened door, looking into a garage which was filled with billowing smoke, injured men and screams of panic.

"I SEE WHAT you mean by taking them off balance," Brunhilde Rojas said. "They're only now setting up security patrols."

The Executioner was silent, peering through a pair of compact electronic binoculars. The digital zoom on the small device made it possible to pick up the smallest of details at a hundred and fifty yards, which was where he had parked their ride.

From the car, they had a slight elevation on Herrera's livery, and Bolan could see a small army of Soldados moving around, gathering supplies, arming up, checking for weaknesses around the perimeter.

The livery served as a cover through which the SNC could launder cocaine money, but Herrera's varied fleet of vehicles was more than just a front. Villanueva had told Bolan that the frames of many of these cars and trucks were packed with drugs, but this garage was also a transportation hub for the Soldados. As such, Bolan was more than happy to take this juicy piece of fruit and smash it to a pulp.

"Let's not give them any more time to get ready for us," Bolan said.

"Grenade launcher?" Rojas guessed.

Bolan nodded. "We strike from a distance and soften them up. Go for each of the vehicles, and try to take out more than one with each grenade. Right now, we don't have to worry too much about direct casualties and antipersonnel operations."

"There'll be enough fuel in there to do half of our work for us, right?" she said.

"Exactly."

They got out of their rental car and went around to the trunk. Bolan had packed two six-shot 40 mm grenade launchers. Together, the weapons had more than enough firepower to take on a small tank.

"First six shots, go for maximum vehicle destruction," Bolan told Rojas. "That will cause enough secondary mayhem and distraction for us to move in closer and finish the job. The last thing I want is for any of that livery to survive and end up going to another cartel at auction. No one gets those trucks… or anything else on the premises."

Rojas nodded, picking up one of the launchers and shouldering it. Bolan grabbed the other. The weapon's scope gave him a good view of their targets below. With the two handles and a collapsible stock measured for his length of pull, the Milkor MGL felt *good*.

Rojas picked out two SUVs parked near each other.

"Just say when," she whispered.

"Now," Bolan said.

Rojas pulled the trigger, and the Milkor thumped against her shoulder, a 40 mm shell arcing through the air and landing just inside the open door of the SUV.

An instant later, both of the black armored vans detonated. The blast was loud and long. Despite the distance, Bolan felt the ground vibrate beneath them.

Bolan looked for something else to hit with the

MGL and chose a pack of motorcycles parked near the garage entrance. As the SUVs belched out gouts of flame and shrapnel, some of Herrera's men ran toward them. Bolan held his fire just long enough for the Soldados to get within a few feet of the motorcycles, and then pumped out a grenade.

The motorbikes flew away from each other, their ruptured gas tanks spraying fuel, which rapidly ignited, thanks to the spark of the grenade. Flames blossomed and washed across the group of men and the remaining motorcycles.

Rojas fired again and struck a moving van in its covered trailer, the 40 mm shell easily puncturing the metal skin and then detonating inside.

She swung and punched another shell into the windshield of a limousine that was starting up, gunmen lunging to get into the war wagon and ride it into bloody battle with their attackers. The 40 mm shell turned the windshield white with dozens of fractures, and passenger windows popped outward.

Bolan turned his attention back to his own sights, seeking more targets around the livery. As his launchers spewed death and devastation into the livery, he could hear Rojas chuckling as she unleashed her last three shots.

Once his MGL was empty, Bolan plucked additional shells from a pouch on his battle harness and fed them into the under-barrel attachment on his rifle. Rojas had just dumped out her empty casings and had replaced them with six more grenades. She punched another shell through the windscreen of a semi truck, blowing its roof and doors off, flame spilling through any opening. Several of Herrera's men were taken out by the blast.

Bolan thumbed his rounds into the M4's "boom tube" one at a time, methodically firing high explosives into the group below.

"Finish your payload," he told Rojas. "We're moving in now!"

Rojas smiled with devilish glee and aimed at another semi just behind the livery, popping off two shots. The twin grenades fell like raindrops but landed with the effect of thunderbolts, the double explosion rupturing the trailer and the cab and causing severe damage to that side of the garage.

As they sprinted back to the car, Bolan scanned the smoldering livery, taking stock of the damage. They dropped their MGLs back in the trunk, and Bolan stuffed an M4 carbine into Rojas's hands as she slithered into the three-point sling.

"Clean kills," he ordered. "That's 5.56, not .300, so we can scavenge ammunition from down there."

Rojas nodded.

Bolan squeezed her shoulder, locking eyes with her.

"Clean. Kills."

Rojas frowned.

"I saw what you did to Macco, remember?" Bolan said.

Rojas shrugged. "We're in a fight. I'll stop them and drop them as quickly as I can. Just as you would."

She turned and shouldered her carbine, looking through the ACOG mounted on the flattop Picatinny rail. A couple of gunmen were rushing up the hill, having finally figured out where the grenades were coming from. Rojas tugged the trigger, ripping a short burst into one of the Soldados and dropping him like a sack of garbage. Bolan picked off the second guy.

"Go time," he grunted.

Even as they descended and crossed the hundred and fifty yards between their grenadier's roost and the garage, the Executioner was taking out enemies. By the time they'd reached the edge of the compound, he had gone through two thirty-round magazines.

He pulled a fragmentation grenade and loaded it into his under-barrel launcher. He signaled to Rojas to take cover, then fired the shell at the chain link around the livery. They both dove into a drainage ditch just in time to avoid the spray of high-velocity shrapnel and broken chain link.

As soon as the bomb popped, Bolan rose, M4 loaded, scanning for further targets through the hole in the fence.

More men were screaming and bleeding on the tarmac, their flesh punctured and lacerated by the shattered fence and Bolan's fragger. He saw a gunman reach for his fallen weapon with a bloody hand. The Executioner put three rounds through his head with the carbine, swiftly and surely.

Rojas was blasting away beside him. He spared her a glance, and she looked to him, as if seeking approval. He was satisfied with La Brujah's display of precision and finality when it came to cutting down the Cali assassins.

"Good. Clean," Bolan said, nodding.

A few moments later, the area grew quiet, the flames of the most recent explosion dying down and all the men in sight down for the count.

"This…seems disappointing," Rojas said, reloading her rifle. "For as dangerous as these guys were, for all the people they've hit for the cartels…"

"Down!" Bolan snapped, catching a glint of light from the corner of his eye.

With lightning speed, he whirled and ripped off a burst in the direction of the flashy, nickel-plated .45 in Herrera's fist. Bolan and Herrera both shot at the same time, and Rojas let out a grunt as the .45 clipped her in the upper chest. The Executioner cored the Soldados captain through the heart with three rounds. The tri-burst sent the Colombian crashing to the ground in a messy heap.

Bolan turned back toward Rojas, moving quickly to her side as she lay, holding her chest.

"Even with body armor, gunshots hurt," Bolan said, reaching down to take her hand.

Rojas blinked, grimacing. "No cry of worry?"

"You were either dead, and anything I said would have been meaningless, or the armor protected you, and taking time to tell you something could have gotten you killed," Bolan answered.

She rolled her eyes as Bolan pulled her to her feet.

"We need to make certain this area's cleared," he said. "Scavenge magazines and any gear you think you won't mind carrying back to the car. Avoid getting too close to any of the vehicles we blitzed—they could still ignite."

They split up, setting about their task quickly. As he cleared the ground level, Bolan heard Rojas calling him.

"Cooper!"

He ran outside and picked up the unmistakable sound of rotors in the sky, getting closer.

"Get in here," Bolan told Rojas.

She raced into the garage. "Herrera was barely ready…"

"But Herrera wasn't the man in charge of the whole cartel," Bolan returned. "Carbonez knew we'd be coming after Herrera at some point…I guess he figured out we decided to change up our schedule."

Rojas nodded.

The roar of two helicopters made it deadly clear that Los Soldados de Cali Nuevos were on top of their game. And Carbonez was moving in for the kill.

11

Mack Bolan had to give the leader of the SNC some respect. The man had thought ahead far enough to prepare a flying squad in order to bring down the hammer on Bolan and Rojas the next time they attacked. In less than twenty-four hours, Carbonez had lost several major portions of his Cali operations, including Macco's force, over a dozen street-level assassins and Herrera's entire livery crew.

Herrera had obviously passed on the Executioner's grim warning.

Bolan didn't tend to underestimate the intelligence or ability of his opposition. Though he hadn't expected Carbonez to move in with quite this much speed and strength, he'd also been hoping to draw the general out, to gauge what kind of rapid response the criminal could summon. And if Herrera's warn-

ing hadn't been enough, Bolan knew the explosions
at the livery would have been audible for miles.

"You were expecting them to come," Rojas stated.

Bolan nodded. "Thinking ahead of the enemy.
Isn't that what kept you on top in New York?"

"Absolutely." Rojas smiled.

Bolan had a live grenade in the breech of the 40
mm tube attached to his carbine. The warhead on
the little canister was High Explosive Dual Purpose,
capable of producing antipersonnel effects, but also
more than strong enough to punch through a wall or
the shell of a lightly armored vehicle.

The helicopters came into view, two UH-1 Hueys
followed by an MH-6 Little Bird. The Hueys were
traditional and reliable workhorses able to carry up
to a dozen men into action if the ships were stuffed
to the gills. Thankfully, neither bird had door gunners, but the smaller, nimble teardrop-shaped chopper behind them did have weapons pods hanging off
the side. The craft was just as versatile as a Huey—
if not more so. The Little Bird was often used as a
rapid deployment aircraft, getting small squads into
areas where the heavier Hueys would have trouble
landing, and they were equally practical as improvised air-to-ground attack ships.

Bolan pushed Rojas back inside the garage before
diving in himself. The tarmac where they'd been
standing was torn up by dozens of rounds raining
from the sky. A few yards to their left, more rounds

blasted apart a section of wall, leaving a ragged opening in the structure.

"What the fuck was that?" Rojas snapped, shocked at the sudden appearance of a hole large enough to drive an SUV through.

"Heavy firepower," Bolan said. "Stay in cover over there, by the tool lockers. Let the fight come to you."

"And you?" Rojas asked.

"I'm going into my element," the Executioner returned.

In an instant, Bolan was through the hole blasted in the wall.

The dual Hueys hovered as their backup bird orbited the livery, ready to lay down even more cover fire. Ropes dropped from the troop ships, unraveling and twisting from the open side doors as the Colombian pilots steadied their charges. The MH-6 circled, and a door gunner fired rounds into the sides of the garage.

The commandos on the Hueys slid deftly down the heavy cords. With the gunship providing close air support, it was clear to Bolan that none of the sixteen men felt vulnerable on their descent.

Despite the heavy firepower wielded by both the Little Bird's gunman and the chopper's 23 mm chain guns, Bolan was banking on a simple fact working in his favor. They wouldn't be prepared for the Executioner's unconventional tactics.

He'd seen the rapid rain of lead coming down

from the door-mounted minigun, which meant that he definitely couldn't waste a second. The MH-6 was loaded and ready, and he led the high-flying aircraft by a few degrees of windage and fired the grenade launcher on his rifle. The gun chugged against his shoulder.

For a moment, he couldn't tell if the shell had made contact. Then, two hundred feet up, the detonation of the HEDP round against the side of the Little Bird gave him all the proof he needed. Smoke began billowing from one of the engine cowlings, which wasn't ideal. He'd been hoping to hit the passenger cabin. Even so, the flight of the MH-6 was erratic, the pilot struggling to keep the bird airborne. And there was no sign of the door gunner.

Bolan turned and saw Rojas in action, putting rounds into the first two of the Colombian gun thugs through the garage doors, 5.56 mm rounds slicing across the distance between them in the blink of an eye.

She'd waited until they were inside, just as he'd ordered her to. From his vantage point, he was well out of her line of fire, and she was safe from any of his shots. Bolan put the M4 on full-auto and cut loose with a long burst into the crowd of startled commandos still milling around in the driveway. As they'd been stacking up to storm Rojas and anyone else who might be assisting her inside, they'd made themselves vulnerable to the Executioner's angle. The carbine snarled out its deadly message at eight-hundred rounds per minute, 5.56 mm rounds slashing through the Soldados.

Bolan swept the group with a figure eight that emptied half of the magazine, and as soon as he let off the trigger, he shifted his focus back to the gunship. The Little Bird was still in the air. It had only been a few seconds since he'd hit it with the grenade, but the men on board seemed to have lost interest in laying down cover fire for the troops below. Bolan ejected the empty casing from his grenade launcher and fed in another 40 mm blaster, priming the rifle in one fluid motion.

Now it was time to take care of the other helicopters.

Bolan's aim was much more certain this time. He pulled the trigger, and a heartbeat later, the cockpit of one of the hovering Hueys disappeared in a bloom of fire and black smoke. The chopper lurched violently, and without anyone to control it, the disabled aircraft was at the mercy of the still-spinning rotors.

The Huey began spiraling toward the ground, and the other pilot pulled up hard, swinging his helicopter around to avoid a deadly crash. It was a deft bit of evasion and skilled flying, but the dangling ropes were still attached to the aircraft, and the spiraling ship snarled into them.

As the disabled helicopter became tangled in the other Huey's ropes, the rotors tugged in one direction while the tail of the bird whipped the opposite way. The twin engines of the functioning chopper revved higher, much higher, and the ropes snapped, sending the disabled bird into its final plummet.

The pilot hadn't been ready for that. The engines were working overtime, and the pilot had been trying to fly the chopper higher to avoid being dragged down with its counterpart. As the ropes came apart, the remaining Huey suddenly upended, looking for a moment as if it were standing on its tail before succumbing to gravity.

The first troop ship hit the livery lot, its rotors shattering into a million pieces as it sliced at the ground. The already flaming chassis produced a secondary explosion, the engines receiving a traumatic impact that tore fuel lines. Gas met overheated metal, and in moments the helicopter spread out a perimeter of flame, a wall racing outward at hundreds of miles an hour and sending the paramilitary force scrambling for cover.

"Rojas!" Bolan called out.

"Damn! What did you—"

That was all Rojas had time to say before they were cut off from each other by the hammer blow of the second Huey slamming itself into the ground.

Bolan ran around the corner of the garage, pausing to reloaded before bringing the M4 up to his shoulder. Over the front sight, he made out the strewn and scattered survivors of the fast-rope team, still recovering from the mayhem of two crashing and burning helicopters.

Bolan punched short bursts into those who were

on their feet, weapons still in hand, precision rounds tearing through heads or slashing through hearts and rib cages.

Carbonez's counterattack would have overwhelmed any force that hadn't expected it. Fortunately, the Executioner had planned for this contingency. He'd been counting on it, wanting Los Soldados de Cali Nuevos to come back and try to hit him with everything they had.

The Soldados had thought they could take their quarry by surprise, but using cover and years of marksmanship skill, Mack Bolan had come out on top.

And yet, for all the carnage he and Rojas had wrought, the Little Bird was still limping along. The craft, bleeding off smoke and fire, swung into view. A body dangled from one side of the helicopter. It was the door gunner in his harness; he had either been taken out by shrapnel or by smoke inhalation. The aircraft wobbled, struggling to stay straight as the chain gun on the far side of the craft roared in defiance. 23 mm shells smashed into the garage roof, shearing huge chunks out of it.

Bolan spotted Rojas racing toward him, darting around falling debris.

"I thought you were good with that thing," Rojas complained. She was smeared with dirt, her short hair wild and scraggly.

"The gunner's out of commission," Bolan said. He pushed another 40 mm shell into the launcher and tracked the teardrop-shaped helicopter as it circled back again.

Bolan fired another HEDP shell into the windshield of the little gunship, and this time, the glass bubble burst. The helicopter rocked as its pilot was obliterated by a sheet of molten copper. The grenade tore into the back of the aircraft and trashed the engine compartment. Bolan grabbed Rojas's hand, and they sprinted inside the garage. As damaged as the livery building was, it was still the best protection from the gutted gunship as it nosed into the tarmac, erupting in an earth-shaking blow that almost rocked Rojas off her feet.

Bolan held on to his ally, keeping her upright.

She leaned against him, eyes wide.

"You do this often?" she asked him.

"Only on days that end with Y," Bolan returned. "Though, this was particularly hairy."

"You have a gift for understatement," Rojas returned, pushing away so she could stand on her own. Through the open garage doors, she observed the wreckage of one of the three helicopters. "I hope Carbonez was in there."

"I doubt we're that lucky," Bolan answered. "He sent out a death squad, and these boys weren't coming in light, despite how fast we took them down."

"Fast," Rojas murmured.

Bolan could tell that she was experiencing the dissonance between intense violence and perception of time. Over the years, he'd developed an easy familiarity with the heightened sense of awareness and sharp reflexes necessary to survive in battle. He understood how, in combat, time seemed to stretch and warp, allowing a trained mind to capture nuances that were normally imperceptible. But countless battles had honed Bolan's internal clock.

"This was only a few minutes. About fifteen, since we started hammering Herrera's cars up on that hill," Bolan told her. "It might have seemed longer…"

Rojas's mouth dropped open.

"Let's get moving. It'll take us a minute to get back to the car," Bolan said. "Grab magazines and whatever else you think will work well for us."

Rojas nodded.

Bolan replenished his ammunition, then glanced up. The columns of smoke rising from the smoldering helicopters and all the other vehicles they'd blown up on this lot would be visible for miles. The day was clear, blue and bright, and now the greasy smears drifted upward, bearing silent witness to the destruction that the Executioner and La Brujah had wrought.

Bolan scanned the sky for aircraft but didn't see anything. He knew the smoke could obscure a high-flying ship, though, so he listened for the slap of rotors or the drone of a plane.

All was quiet for the moment, so he and Rojas returned to their rental vehicle. Rojas had loaded up a bag with 5.56 mm ammunition, and she had found several hand grenades which hadn't been destroyed in the conflict.

She had also taken a couple of tactical radios off of the dead commandos. Bolan smiled at her prescience, as he'd grabbed one, as well. The frequencies and encryption might be changed soon, but for now, they could listen in on Carbonez's radio network.

Bolan plugged an earpiece in and listened to the chatter. Though he understood enough Spanish to get by and could pass on simple messages, the men on the line were going a mile a minute.

Rojas chuckled.

"What's funny?" Bolan asked.

Rojas pointed to her radio. "Carbonez is losing his mind. He's trying to get more details and is becoming frustrated by ground crews who've lost contact with the ships."

They were nearly to the car when they heard distant sirens.

The fires in the livery complex were growing and spreading, and Bolan hoped that Villanueva had warned the Cali fire department about the possibility of tertiary explosions at the site, due to cooked off ammunition.

It was time to return to the safe house.

12

By the time Bolan spotted the drone, it was too late. They were already halfway back to the safe house when a flicker, a shadow crossing the sun, caught his eye. The drone had been flying too high to be spotted back at Herrera's livery, especially with all the smoke in the air.

Villanueva hadn't indicated that the SNC possessed drones, but it wasn't unheard of for cartels to get their hands on that kind of tech. Ironically, Colombia's National Police often used UAVs specifically to interdict drug trafficking. Every once in a while, though, a Boeing ScanEagle would "fall off the back of a truck"—if the price was right and the cop was willing to look the other way.

If this was indeed a ScanEagle on their tail, the good news was that it was just a camera. The ScanEagle was too small to mount air-to-surface missiles.

"Something wrong?" Rojas asked.

"Los Soldados have a drone, and it's following us."

Rojas poked her head out the passenger side window, shielding her eyes as she scanned the skies. "Damn it."

"That's one thing you could say about it," Bolan commented. "I'm going to drive somewhere with a little more clutter between us and the drone. When I say so, you get out and fall back to the secondary safe house."

"What about you?"

Bolan considered the possibilities before answering. "We let them hit the safe house. With me in it."

"That's suicide, isn't it?" Rojas asked. "After all—"

"After all, it's one of me against a bunch of them," Bolan cut her off.

"I'm only trying to show some concern," she snapped. "I'm worried what kind of contingencies you have in place if you get killed."

Bolan smirked. "Wondering if I'll send someone else after you? You're in Colombia, where half the cartels in the country sent hit men to greet you at the airport."

"Those I'll be expecting," she retorted.

"Listen, you've risked your life four times since yesterday morning. You've paid your dues…"

"For every murder?" Rojas pressed.

"Enough that if we get through this, no one else—no one in the States, at least—will come after you."

"Fine. But if the Soldados take you out of the game, how am I supposed to finish what we started?"

"There's money and supplies at the backup safe house," Bolan told her.

"Money?" Rojas asked.

"To hire guns, to get other cartels on your side. Just enough to bring down the SNC permanently, if you do it right. There are diagrams and tactical information there, too, to make you invaluable to the other groups."

"And what if I decide to take that money and run, instead?"

"Sooner or later, the friends I have will pay a visit to Cali. And if you are unlucky enough to meet them, do yourself a favor and eat a bullet," Bolan said.

They were approaching an overpass and slowed as he drove beneath it, pausing at the curb. "Get moving. I have an ambush to set for Carbonez's troops."

Rojas began to open the door but paused, locking eyes with him. Bolan knew she wanted to trust him, wanted to believe this wouldn't end with her back in jail—or dead on the streets of Cali. He'd played his hand, but he couldn't give her any guarantees. La Brujah would have to accept that and come to her own conclusions.

"This plan will work best if I'm on my own," Bolan said firmly. "Wait until I contact you, and then move on to the next location."

Rojas stepped out of the car but stuck her head back in before closing the door.

"Kill them all," she said. "Then come to me. We will finish Carbonez. *Together.*"

Bolan pulled back into traffic and accelerated.

The Executioner was throwing a housewarming party, and he planned to welcome his guests with his own brand of cleansing fire.

CARBONEZ STOOD IN the computer center at his offices, watching the live footage from the SNC's unmanned aerial vehicle. It was a clone of the Boeing Insitu ScanEagle, with more than a few proprietary features stripped from its system. Even so, it was more than sufficient to keep track of La Brujah and her American friend.

Carbonez frowned, arms crossed, his eyes unblinking as he tracked the moving sedan across the screen.

At first, the Colombian kingpin had been wondering if this pair's exploits had been exaggerated, if Macco's crew and the street assassins had simply not been the ruthless, capable soldiers Carbonez believed them to be. But as he'd seen the assault on Herrera unfold, his doubts about the strength of his opposition began to fade.

They'd managed to destroy *three* of the SNC's helicopters. He'd lost six million dollars in an instant, and that was just from the Hueys. The MH-6 was worth another five-hundred thousand, give or take, for both the airframe and the powerful armaments. Not to mention all the vehicles they'd taken out with their grenade launchers. The destruction had been hard to sit through, but Carbonez was glad for the presence of the ScanEagle.

Now, it was on the hunt, trailing the pair in their car. Wherever those two laid their heads—and they would need a rest, after the brutal battle they'd waged—he would find them and bring them down.

Carbonez was getting tired of being on the defensive. This time, he wasn't fucking around.

"Sir?"

Carbonez had been so lost in his thoughts and anger, he was startled by the drone operator's voice. "What is it?"

"They stopped under an overpass for a moment," the man told him. "But they're moving again."

"So what?" Carbonez asked.

"We can either watch the overpass, or we can follow the car," the operator explained. "As good as we have it with the ScanEagle, we can't keep an eye on them both, if they split up."

The general focused in on the sedan as it merged with traffic on the other side of the overpass. "Keep it hovering there for a minute. We've got the make, model and general direction of the car. We can afford to drop it for a few minutes. Let's see if one of them stayed behind."

The operator nodded.

Could someone have seen the drone? The wingspan was just a little over ten feet, and operating over ten-thousand feet in the air, the ScanEagle was supposed to be low profile. It was highly unlikely that anyone would notice it with the naked eye. Not even a witch.

"Coming up on two minutes," the operator announced. Two minutes, and no one had emerged.

But what kind of wait would that be to a woman who'd spent seven years in prison? Carbonez had been behind bars himself, and one thing that a person learned in prison was that you had to be patient. Waiting was your friend.

The operator looked to Carbonez for confirmation, then pulled the drone off the overpass, swinging back toward the sedan.

It didn't take long for the operator to pinpoint the vehicle with the ScanEagle, and Carbonez took a deep, cleansing breath. His neck was stiff, shoulders aching from the tension of waiting for…what?

Why *would* they separate? Why not just ditch the car, stick together, and shake the tail?

Or would they split up in order to draw Carbonez and his men into yet another trap? The last time the SNC had thought they had the American and the Witch where they wanted them, it had ended in devastation. He couldn't even hope to count the casualties, let alone the drugs and weapons stored at Herrera's. The cost of this day alone could top ten million dollars.

The decimation of Macco's crew was another

hemorrhage of money and manpower, and Carbonez was already hearing reports that opportunistic cartels were vying to secure that part of Cali for their own. All of El Tiburon's efforts to maintain SNC control there had been for naught.

Maddening.

Carbonez stepped away from the monitors, brushing his fingers through his short hair.

"That is how he does it," Carbonez murmured.

"Sir?"

"That's how he gets under the skin of his opponents. He plans ahead. He leaves what seem like glaring holes in his defenses, or tries to lull you into believing there's a blind spot in his tactics. He exposes himself just enough to be a tantalizing target."

And once this American's opponents stepped into the open, he turned the tables and slammed the jaws of his trap shut. When the man attacked, he used the momentum, the sloth of larger forces against themselves, and no matter how fast a small unit could adapt, none could move, or think, as quickly as this lone warrior.

But so far, this man and his wicked ally didn't seem to be aware of the drone following them. Luck might be with the SNC, and they wouldn't be expecting Carbonez to summon up more forces so soon after the devastation at the livery.

"All right, get some men up and ready for action," Carbonez ordered the lieutenant who'd been stand-

ing by at the back of the room. "Who do we have
that we can deploy against these two?"

"I'll get you a list. How big a force do you want
to send?" the man asked.

"How big can we assemble inside of an hour?"
Carbonez shot back. "I want everyone, and I want all
the firepower you can manage. I don't care if we've
got a hundred guys there—I want to use every bullet in our inventory. Every grenade. Every rocket.
We're not fucking around here."

"Right, sir."

The drone operator spoke up. "They stopped off
at a bodega. La Brujah must be driving because the
man got out of the passenger side and went in."

Carbonez leaned over the operator's shoulder.
"You're certain?"

"Yes. Probably getting provisions. They'd need
water after being so close to so much flame."

Carbonez nodded. "Just see if you can spot the
driver from the window."

BOLAN'S SHOPPING TRIP was one of necessity. Heading into the bodega, his first order of business was
to pick up a package of garbage bags and a roll of
duct tape. He needed to maintain the illusion that
he wasn't alone in the sedan, so he had to make it
look as if both he and Rojas were entering their safe
house.

It wouldn't take long to inflate a couple of bags
and tape them together to resemble a human form,

and he'd throw a jacket on top to complete the effect. He glanced around the bodega and found a cheap baseball cap that would also help hide the mannequin's true nature. Moving through the small shop, Bolan paused long enough to spot a shelf of wigs for women.

"Excuse me," Bolan asked the man behind the counter. "Can I purchase the foam heads as well as the wigs?"

"Si," the man said.

Bolan chose the one that most resembled Rojas's hair. From the ScanEagle footage, it would be almost impossible for the enemy to make out details like hair color, but Bolan figured he was better safe than sorry. He didn't want to give Carbonez any grounds for suspicion.

Next, Bolan surveyed the fridge full of cold drinks. He chose four large water bottles—he needed to hydrate after the heat and adrenaline of battle, but more importantly, he could use the empty bottles to give his dummy legs.

Finally, he grabbed a pair of cheap plastic shoes and some pantyhose and carried his basket up to the cash.

"Planning a party?" the clerk asked in Spanish, raising an eyebrow.

"You have no idea," Bolan answered, paying for his goods. "Thanks. Keep the change."

Bolan returned to the car, his supplies hidden in paper bags. He slid into the passenger seat. He'd left his jacket, sleeve stuffed with newspaper, leaning on the driver's window to make it seem as if the car was occupied.

Bolan tugged the jacket to one side and climbed in behind the wheel. The bags would take up space on the other seat, masking the lack of a passenger.

Bolan drove away from the bodega, already scanning for another secluded spot to pull over. He needed time away from the drone's watchful eye to assemble his dummy. Another overpass loomed ahead, and once beneath it, Bolan cut the engine. He stuffed the panty hose, first with the plastic shoes to form feet, then drank one bottle of water and emptied the others. He slid them into the nylon legs, applying duct tape to keep everything together. Then he blew into a garbage bag, forming a "torso" about the size of Rojas's, and attached the limbs.

He added the foam head, wig and baseball cap using more tape. The jacket went around her "shoulders."

When the SNC came knocking, they would be expecting two people.

And Bolan planned to give them an easy target.

13

The ScanEagle lived up to its name, giving Carbonez and his troops a sharp, bird's-eye view of the safe house. It was out past the shanty towns and close to the river. Few people lived in this area because of all the sewage and refuse that flowed out of Cali and ended up here.

The safe house was an isolated little building by the water. No civilians were likely to wander out this way, and the general was glad for that. The Soldados enjoyed a certain amount of public support because their war was with the Colombian government, in all its corruption and incompetence. Openly engaging in violence against Cali's citizens would only damage the SNC's standing with the folks who had been there to shield him, and would be again. Though Carbonez didn't give a flying shit about these people, their loyalty was too useful a resource to squander.

Carbonez watched the sedan pull up to the house. The American exited the passenger seat and walked to the driver's side, lifting…well, obviously that was the woman, no? She appeared to have been injured during the fight, though that hadn't been apparent in the wake of the battle. The details of their exfiltration had been obscured by the smoke pouring from wrecked vehicles and the crumbled livery building.

The man was supporting her as they walked toward the front door, her head resting on his shoulder.

"So that's why they stopped at the bodega for supplies," Carbonez said. "He wanted to give her first aid in the car. I guess her driving ability wasn't hindered…"

"No," the drone operator said. "But she might have taken a shot to the leg. An injury in one leg wouldn't have impaired her driving ability, and that would have explained some of the long stops as he treated her."

Carbonez wished he could see their faces better, but the resolution from fifteen-thousand feet was only so good.

"We've sent exact coordinates and routes to the field team," the operator told Carbonez. "We'll keep an eye on the house, just in case someone leaves, or if they seem to be fortifying against an attack. So far, they haven't shown any sign that they've spotted the ScanEagle or that they're headed home to do anything but rest and recuperate." The operator hesitated. "Will you be…going in with them?" he asked.

Carbonez frowned. He wanted to be a part of this attack, but his days of being a frontline commander were long past. He was no longer in his prime, or even close. Still, there were things he could do from here as easily as he could on site.

"No," he answered. "I wish, though. It would be glorious. This will have to be my seat for the show."

The operator nodded.

Carbonez kept his eyes on the safe house. The American and the Witch were in his crosshairs now, and he didn't dare blink.

The American knew how to draw in his enemies, make them push to the limits of their attack, and then blindside them. Carbonez had to watch from afar. That had its benefits. The ScanEagle would be the closest he could ever get to being an omniscient battlefield observer. With the communications at this command center, he could steer and manipulate the war against these two interlopers.

And the best part of all? The American had placed himself exactly where Carbonez wanted him. The general had no compunctions about cutting loose with everything he had.

MACK BOLAN DUMPED his mannequin just inside the door and slammed it shut. The shades were already drawn. He went back out and moved the car into the carport, which was made from scrap siding that had washed up on the shore of the Cauca River.

Bolan glanced out across the sluggish water. Real

estate along the Cauca's banks was not much sought after. Over half a dozen gold mines emptied their silt and waste into the river, and at the end of the millennium, the SNC's predecessors had engaged in a killing spree under the guise of "cleansing."

The name of this atrocity was *Cali limpia, Cali linda*—Clean Cali, Beautiful Cali—and thousands of prostitutes, homeless people, street children and homosexuals had been callously murdered and dumped into the river. Cities had gone broke from the cost of retrieving bodies and conducting autopsies.

Bolan was fully aware of Cali's trials and tribulations, the nation of Colombia beset by narcotics-funded terrorism and civil unrest. He'd been here many times, and sometimes it seemed that, no matter how much of a dent he put in the hordes of gunmen and thugs, there was always some group of maniacs bringing torment and ruin to honest, innocent people.

He was reminded of a saying about baby alligators in a swamp. Though they would eventually grow to become dominant, apex predators, the gators started out in huge clutches of eggs, and when they hatched, they were the smallest, easiest prey in the wetlands. They grew up avoiding being eaten by bigger creatures, and by the time they reached adulthood, the reptiles had learned only one lesson. Eat or be eaten. The surviving gators made up for the fear and terror inflicted upon them by devouring everything that had tried to eat them when they were small.

Bolan knew the cycle of violence was difficult,

almost impossible, to break. And Colombia wasn't the only corner of the world crippled by corruption, suffering and brutality. Poverty, shattered families, the cycle of predation was something that required so much more than a carefully placed .44 Magnum or a packet of C-4. Colombia needed an honest government, better education and jobs for everyone. But Bolan had his own part to play in weeding out the evil in this country, and he would see it through to the end.

Any Soldados who survived this conflict would relate the horrors of their encounter with the Executioner, passing on the details of his lethal crusade as a warning to others who would dare follow in the SNC's footsteps.

Bolan checked the laser trip wires that he'd set around the perimeter of the property, one of the reasons that he felt comfortable with fully drawn curtains. Satisfied, he returned to the house.

Once inside, he took out his PDA and sent a text to Stony Man.

Expecting company en masse. Need eyes in the sky.

Either Kurtzman would make use of a spy satellite watching South America, or he'd commandeer one of Colombia's legitimate ScanEagle drones to provide real-time information on what was approaching.

In the meantime, Bolan was prepared. He'd brought in both of the Milkor MGLs as well as his M-203-equipped M4 carbine. He wanted as much of a force equalization as he could get, and there was nothing like 40 mm packages of high explosives to balance the odds between one man and a deadly army.

The M4 and its launcher would be strapped across his back. He'd load one MGL with buckshot rounds, turning the launcher into a 40 mm shotgun, belching out a swarm of hundreds of quarter-inch pellets in a flesh-shredding wave of damnation. He'd fill the other with fragmentation rounds.

Bolan went to what would have been the laundry room and quickly pulled out two panels from the lower part of the wall. There was a tunnel behind that, which led into a drainage ditch that Bolan and Rojas had spent their first day transforming into a camouflaged passageway. Using tarps and a lattice of sticks and boards, they'd covered the ditch and then spread and smoothed out dirt to make it hard to see. Bolan bagged up the MGLs and his M4 and crawled out to the river's edge where there was plenty of scrub and brush to hide in. From there, he could flank and ambush the assault force moving in on the safe house.

He darted quickly back through the tunnel and reentered the safe house.

"Cooper?" It was Bolan's hands-free set, Rojas calling him.

"You got some news for me from that radio you borrowed?" Bolan asked.

"And then some," Rojas said. "The chatter might have been a bit fast for you to follow…"

"You noticed."

Rojas chuckled. "Basically, you're going to have about a hundred visitors, and they've been told to make certain that the safe house is turned to sawdust before they dare to make a move on it."

"I figured as much," Bolan returned.

Rojas sounded a bit confused with the next question. "How the hell did you convince them that I wasn't able to walk?"

"I made a dummy out of some panty hose, plastic bags and duct tape," Bolan replied.

"Duct tape," Rojas murmured. "Listen, if you don't have things all set up, you might want to hurry," Rojas warned.

"Thanks for the concern. Keep me updated on anything new," Bolan said.

"Will do."

Bolan retrieved another piece of Colombian military equipment, some more ordnance that had "fallen off of an army transport." This was an M60 general-purpose light machine gun. It was a classic old design, having been replaced by the even more veteran FN MAG in the United States military, but the Executioner was skilled and familiar with the Pig, as it was nicknamed, and he could handle the extra weight.

Firing five hundred and fifty NATO rounds per minute, the M60 was everything Bolan needed in

terms of raw stopping power and enemy suppression.
He knew the recoil intimately, so he could adjust his
aim to remain on target for long bursts. He also had
a second-nature familiarity with the trigger, allowing him to put out two- and three-round bursts to
make the most of each belt without having to reload.

If the SNC were ready to unleash every ounce of
firepower they could arrange, then the Executioner
was going to need the very best of his own arsenal.

He checked his PDA.

Sure enough, Kurtzman had gotten ahold of an of-
ficial, active-duty Colombian ScanEagle. It was cir-
cling at nineteen-thousand feet over the safe house,
and its cameras relayed the sight of an armed convoy of pickup trucks, SUVs and other vehicles. The
pickups had improvised machine gun mounts, and
there was a flatbed tractor-trailer with an array of
60 mm and 81 mm mortars on the back.

"Is it go time, Bear?" Bolan asked.

"Yeah. We estimate it'll take them about five minutes to set up and start slamming you," Kurtzman
replied. "We've been listening in on your conversation with Rojas, too. She's telling you the truth
about what she heard on the radio, according to our
translations."

"Thanks, but I didn't doubt her," Bolan said.

"You would have been chewing me out if I didn't
confirm it for you," Kurtzman countered.

Bolan managed a smile. "Those mortars are what
worry me the most. I wasn't expecting them."

"It looks like Carbonez called in some favors from the FARC or some other communist insurgent group," Kurtzman informed him. "That's where the artillery came from."

"Well, I inspired them with my own heavy explosives assault," Bolan noted. "I reap what I've sown."

"I'll let you get moving, then. The live feed will keep for as long as you need it. The ScanEagle was just launched, so it's got at least 20 hours of staying power," Kurtzman promised.

Bolan thanked him, then piled his M60 and the ammunition belts on to a drag bag and crawled back into the exit ditch. It didn't take long for the enemy to begin their assault. He was three quarters of the way through the hidden tunnel when the ground shuddered with the first detonations of high-explosive mortar shells—60 mm and 81 mm artillery rounds were capable of amazing devastation in an antipersonnel role.

Right now, Bolan had to play a waiting game. He hunched inside the passageway, watching from the ScanEagle footage on his PDA the destruction unleashed by the New Soldiers' convoy. The crews were simply hammering the safe house.å

The building was swallowed up by a black cloud of smoke as the ambush force cut loose without any warning. The earth shook around the Executioner in his foxhole. He recalled that concentrated mortar fire was often more than sufficient to clean out packs of enemies dug into tunnels, that the lighter

60 mm mortars had been used to deadly effect in
World War II.

That was in the '40s, and the SNC had twenty-first
century ammunition. Bolan hoped that here, seventy
yards away from the safe house, he was not going
to catch a shell right on top of him. Fortunately, the
Colombian artillery crews didn't seem interested
in bombing anything more than the building itself.
Bolan continued slithering along, stopping when he
reached the end of the tunnel. He peered left and
right along the shore. He could have checked with
the ScanEagle, but it offered a less than ideal view
of the riverfront.

Besides, Bolan didn't want to come to rely on
technology completely. Part of the reason why he
was so effective was that he could switch between
his own senses and advanced electronic optics. That
flexibility was exactly how he could outthink and
outmaneuver the enemy. He didn't treat any problem
the same way because each situation came with its
own context and contingencies.

Sure enough, the warrior saw a small squad making its way along the embankment. They had their
own hands-free sets. He switched his device over to
the frequency they'd gotten from the captured radios at the livery. This group was patrolling for any
hiding spots their quarry might have retreated to.

That meant that sooner or later, they would stum-
ble upon this tunnel. However, since they were in
radio contact with the home base, or at least the ar-

tillery crews, Bolan had to be careful in dealing
with them. He eyed the Cauca river. It was thick
and murky enough that he could sneak up on them,
submerged.

Bolan crept out of the ditch and added the M60
to his cache of weapons in the bushes. He had the
Desert Eagle and suppressed Beretta with him, as
well as an assortment of knives—the ideal arsenal
for eliminating opponents silently, in close quarters.

As the nearby group of Colombian gunmen stood
watching the high explosive shells rain down on the
safe house, Bolan sliced into the foul waters of the
Cauca, disappearing beneath the surface like a crocodile.

It was time to take some prey.

14

Brunhilde Rojas continued to monitor the conversations between Carbonez and his troops with a bud in one ear as she made her way through the streets of Cali.

The city was no stranger to violence erupting in its neighborhoods, but right now, with aircraft bombing office complexes, grenades smashing into trucks and buildings, and helicopters dropping from the sky in flaming fireballs, the world seemed to have come unhinged.

She and Cooper had arrived in the city, and all at once, there was a storm breaking loose. She couldn't even begin to consider how many people they'd killed over the past two days. Yet here she was, with a couple of handguns, listening to the pulse of operations among Los Soldados de Cali Nuevos as they stormed the safe house.

And they were pulling out all of the stops. She'd buzzed Cooper after she heard about some mobile artillery loaded onto a flatbed truck. *Real* artillery, 81 mm and 60 mm mortars borrowed from insurgents. La Brujah and the American had done their absolute best to throw the SNC into panic mode.

She glanced at her smartphone, then sent a message off to the mysterious operators on the other side. Cooper had told her to text "the Farm" if she needed any help in the field when they were separated.

Any way to locate the origin of the radio chatter?

Been working on it since radios acquired.

Progress?

Have coordinates for you.

A link appeared, and she clicked it, opening an aerial map of Cali. She examined it, then frowned. She knew the place. It was formerly a JUNGLA barracks which had been shut down, thanks to a wave of bombings which had convinced the Colombian army to move the unit's headquarters to a more secure location.

Naturally, the bombings had been planned so that the infrastructure of the base was left intact for the very purpose of usurping that facility. Rojas bit her lower lip.

Maybe, just maybe, she could get the drop on the

base. No, she wouldn't be able to stage another assault like the one on the livery. But she could get a nice preview of whatever Carbonez *hadn't* thrown at Cooper and the safe house. Still, it was a risky proposition, and it wouldn't do either her or Cooper any good if Carbonez welcomed her to his headquarters with a bullet to the brain—or worse.

"Cooper's given you more than enough help," Rojas muttered. "You're out of jail, you're back in Colombia and you're armed. Time to take some initiative."

She thought about Cooper's orders. Get to the other safe house.

Their backup would have more guns and another car. She smiled.

She'd go to the other safe house and build up her arsenal, then swing back to Cooper's location and help mop up. After that, they'd hit Carbonez's compound together.

Rojas broke into a jog. She intended to get to the fallback site within ten minutes.

THE MEN ON the shore did not seem to have a clue that Bolan was creeping up on them. He had improvised a snorkel with a piece of tubing, and he'd slipped on protective goggles to keep his vision clear and his eyes safe from possible infection as he swam. Using a silent crawl stroke, he caught up to the patrol group and made his way slowly up the incline of the shore. Fortunately, he didn't have anything

to fear from local creatures, either catfish or croco-
diles. The water was rank and polluted, and when he
rose from the murky muck, he knew that he'd bear
a distinct odor as he eased into position behind the
nearest Soldado.

The four men chuckled and cheered, watching
their comrades pound the safe house with artillery
shells. The quartet were acting like they were at a *futbol* match, not in the middle of a military operation.

The Executioner was about to end the celebration.
He drew the suppressed Beretta and rose from the
Cauca river. In one smooth movement, he executed
one of the gunmen with a 9 mm pill to the base of
his skull, the sound of the shot easily lost in the rattle
and roar of angry mortar shells.

There was now a crater where the safe house had
been. Carbonez was not taking any chances with the
people who had shot his helicopters out of the sky
and decimated his troops. Still, the barrage was last-
ing much longer than necessary to destroy a simple
shack by the river.

One of the patrolmen noticed his friend topple
face-first to the ground, the back of his head a bloody
crater from the impact of a 9 mm slug. The Colombian started to turn, but Bolan popped him through
the left ear, a sizzling quick slug scrambling that
man's brains.

Two troopers down, Bolan reholstered the Beretta and drew his combat knife. The transition was
swift as he closed in on the Colombian gangster man-

ning a radio. The Soldado finished reporting another wave of direct hits and lowered the handset from his lips. Bolan clamped one hand over the man's mouth, wrenching his head back as hard as he could. In the next moment, he brought down his wicked combat blade, spearing the man through his throat, sharp steel carving like a guillotine through his windpipe and major blood vessels in one savage slash.

The last of the quartet whirled around, noticing the sudden violent act in his peripheral vision. He started to bring up his rifle as Bolan dumped aside the radio man. With a sharp snap kick, Bolan drove the fourth guy's own rifle into his stomach. The wind knocked out of him, the Soldado bent over, gasping, no longer in control of the gun. With another quick step, Bolan snatched a thick handful of the Colombian's hair, stabilizing his head. The Executioner brought down his combat knife again, this time plunging six inches of lethal steel into the back of his enemy's neck. His spine severed instantly, the gangster collapsed first to his knees, then facedown in the mud.

Four down. And an entire army to go.

Bolan took to the shore and ran back for the Milkor launchers at full speed. Even if the mortar crews were aware that the patrol team had been taken down by the very target they had intended to reduce to his component atoms, they continued hammering at the safe house.

He skidded to a halt by the grenade launchers

and double-checked their loads. The buckshot-filled MGL was a direct line of sight shotgun that was meant for slashing apart groups of enemy soldiers. The HEDP rounds were better for indirect fire. He consulted his PDA again, making certain that the flatbed truck hadn't moved. Sure enough, the mortars were still emplaced, though the live feed from Kurtzman's ScanEagle showed that they'd stopped firing.

Maybe they were out of ammunition. Even so, the pickup truck technicals were cutting loose with their heavy machine guns.

Nope. Carbonez was not leaving anything to chance. Luckily, the embankment and the position of the terrain made it so that Bolan was not in direct line of sight. That was no problem for the Milkor, though. He had the range, and he had the necessary familiarity with the multi-shot launcher to do what needed to be done.

Bolan fired three rapid shots, left to right, shifting only slightly. He wanted to make sure he'd covered the mortar crews. The flight time of the arcing shells would give him the opportunity to adjust aim and fire three more grenades. These three were intended for the technicals with their mounted heavy machine guns—weapons that would overwhelm even the most talented and experienced of warriors, if he entered their line of fire.

He consulted his eye in the sky again, but it turned out to be an unnecessary step. The flatbed truck took a direct hit from Bolan's first three grenades. Within moments, the roar of explosions reached his ears. What had once been a mobile artillery platform was now shredded by detonating 40 mm shells and the secondary explosions of stored 60 mm and 81 mm mortars.

The trailer ignited in a roiling cloud, lit from within by the hot, angry orange flames. Men screamed and scrambled away from the erupting chaos. A few seconds later, Bolan's fourth shell struck, rocking one of the pickup trucks violently. Bolan glanced at his PDA. Compared to the flatbed, this explosion was nothing to write home about, but to the machine gunner on the back of the technical, it was lethal. The gunner was gone in a puff of smoke, body parts littering the ground around the vehicle.

Bolan's next shot missed the other technical, but it landed between two shooters who were lying prone beside it, emptying their rifles into the chaos around them. Shrapnel swept across the riflemen, ending their lives with high-velocity steel severing arteries and destroying vital organs.

The sixth round *was* on target for the pickup truck serving as a third improvised machine gun nest. A 40 mm fist of high explosive ordnance slammed into the pickup, and once again, gunner and the heavy machine gun were turned to ground meat and scrap metal. The thunderbolt was more than sufficient to cause the pickup to collapse on its rear axle, wheels broken off the shaft. Even if the driver had survived, he wouldn't have been able to retreat with the truck.

As the explosions subsided, enemy RPGs and rifles flared to life again in the distance. Still, Bolan could see from the ScanEagle feed that the force had lost much of its superior firepower. Now, the once-disciplined ranks were showing signs of panic. Still, the Soldados continued shooting, hoping to dig out the enemy with gunfire. Above him, thanks to the artillery barrage and countless fires, smoke formed a hazy, thick canopy, blotting out the sky over Bolan's position.

It was a good start, but there was still more work to be done. He opened the Milkor, fed in a new load of six 40 mm grenades and closed the action. He knew approximately where the enemy lines were, and how they had been staggered and broken apart by the initial destruction of their mortar platform.

This time, instead of HEDP rounds, he was going with fragmentation grenades, and he fired them off, spacing each shot by thirty yards. By now, smoke and fire rising from the SNC's ranks made it much more difficult to gauge the effects of the initial volley on the convoy. Bolan was firing to add to their confusion as much as to cut down the opposing force.

The final cleanup was going to be an effort by much more direct lines of fire, at closer range. For that, he'd use the buckshot-loaded Milkor, the M4 and his M60.

He grabbed both weapons, and now that he'd destroyed the SNC's remaining artillery shells, he returned to the tunnel. He loaded his arsenal on to the drag bag and reentered the passageway, which had remained relatively intact despite the assault on the safe house.

Surely, the enemy would have had some indication of where Bolan had been firing from, and if not, the sudden, quiet deaths of four of their forward observers would have them moving their attention to the river's edge. He reserved most of his strength and both hands for crawling through the tunnel, loops around his shoulders and battle harness allowing him to bring along forty-seven pounds of high-impact weaponry, not including belts of ammunition and spare grenades.

He reached a section of the tunnel where the ceiling had been blown off and the passage had partially collapsed, making it difficult to squeeze through. Bolan grabbed several handfuls of dirt and rubbed it into his hair and over his face. Then he raised his head slowly, through the hole in the ceiling. The sun-baked soil would provide him with camouflage, and easing into view rather than making a sudden move would prevent him from catching a Soldado's eye. With the smoke hazing up the sky, there was little danger of being spotted by Carbonez's drone. He glanced at his own PDA to confirm the lack of visibility from the murky sky.

At ground level, he had good lines of sight. And the scattered Colombian gangsters had regrouped.

Several men were walking toward the smoldering crater that used to be the safe house. Anything left inside had been hammered into dust during the merciless artillery barrage. Even so, the troopers approached cautiously.

They had already been stung by a rain of fragmentation grenades and didn't want to make the mistake of underestimating the opposition. In his earbud, Bolan heard the broadcast of a platoon of men at the riverbank, some thirty yards back.

The SNC had discovered the dead patrolmen.

The Executioner had found a nice vantage point, allowing him to observe both the river and the smoldering safe house site. Bolan drew out the Milkor with its six-shot cylinder bearing buckshot loads. He calculated the drop to the river. It was simple to measure and estimate where to aim to achieve the most devastation.

With a surge, Bolan rose high enough to clear his foxhole with the MGL and fired two bursts of buckshot down to the riverbank, right at the platoon. The men hadn't yet spread out to search the shoreline, and one blast hurled four men off of their feet, each guy riddled with dozens of .24 caliber holes, the payload of hundreds of projectiles creating a deadly swarm of flesh-destroying balls. The second blast tore the arm off another man as he and the rest of his squad were inundated with buckshot.

The two pops drew attention from the troops by the crater, but the Executioner whirled swiftly, emp-

tying the other four cylinders at the assembled Soldados. Sprays of buckshot showered the men. As the
first burst erupted from the muzzle of the Milkor, the
Soldados were scrambling, seeking cover. Those too
slow were peppered with copper-jacketed projectiles.
Some were killed instantly, but mostly, Bolan found
that he was hindering his opponents with shrapnel
injuries.

He preferred not to leave people to suffer, but
right now, the odds were so heavily stacked against
him that he needed to use the buckshot to slow down
the enemy as well as to eliminate several of them.
He'd finish the job with the M60, but for now, the
MGL had done exemplary work. He shouldered a
bandolier of buckshot grenades for the M4's grenade
launcher, slung the rifle and brought the Pig to his
shoulder. Through the smoke and haze, the warrior
made out the shapes of armed men and began tapping off short tri-bursts.

Within moments, the remaining Soldados were
running for their lives. Bolan squeezed 7.62 mm
NATO rounds out of the barrel in pairs or trios. Because Bolan was using the M60 as a rifle, the gun
didn't recoil enough to draw rounds off target. As
a result, each shot hit home at full impact, meeting
flesh and bone and tearing through everything in
its path.

Thanks to the confusion and the smoke, Bolan
was able to empty the entire two-hundred-round belt,

leaving dozens of men on the ground, dead or dying in the initial rampage.

Since he hadn't gone all out with the light machine gun, the M60 hadn't produced a massive muzzle flash, especially with the flash hider he'd installed on the Pig's muzzle. With little to give his position away, Bolan was still relatively hidden against the enemy.

The SNC troops were growing more confused by the minute. Men who had been following their comrades down to the river began to open fire. Rifles crackled, sending rounds in Bolan's general direction. Many of these shots continued on toward the group at the crater, and the Colombians who were by the safe house site lost even more composure and discipline as they realized that they were facing both enemy and friendly fire.

Bolan ducked his head low as RPG shells zoomed within feet of his foxhole. From his covered position, he watched as the Soldados, caught up in the fog of war, chewed at each other, the survivors giving in to panic and confusion.

Bolan wasn't going to let his enemy do the whole job, though. He replaced the belt in the M60 and took a few more moments to reload the Milkor MGL with more buckshot rounds. There was no way he was going to leave these thugs in any position to continue their predation on the people of Cali.

Closing the breech of the Milkor, the Executioner checked which side was doing better, and rose, hammering the winners of the exchanges between the confused Soldados de Cali Nuevos.

His mission was almost complete. The Executioner had all but dismantled the SNC, but he wanted to make certain that the survivors remembered the crushing defeat he handed to them today.

15

One moment, Los Soldados de Cali Nuevos were unleashing hell on a level that would have made the forces invading Normandy proud. Under Carbonez's orders, the Soldados had concentrated high explosives on a single target, obliterating it. The attack had been swift and sudden. Even if the Witch and the American had some kind of eye in the sky, they would only have had minutes to prepare.

Then the first of the grenades landed on the flatbed truck, and the tables turned on the SNC. Again.

Carbonez watched that first series of violent explosions unfold, then a second, then a third. Pallets of extra shells for the mortars were shaken so hard they detonated. The explosions surged and flowed, growing into an even greater rumbling set of blasts, fire and shrapnel sweeping away from the destroyed trailer bed, killing and maiming dozens of men around the vehicle. From his position in the command room, looking through the eyes of his Scan-Eagle, the general watched his victory snatched away and hurled into the jaws of defeat.

Somewhere, under the cover of a column of dust and smoke churning the sky, making the ground and river invisible to the drone, the American and the Witch were working their devilish magic, combining their powers in a counterstrike that was at once merciless and surprising. Veins stood out on Carbonez's forehead.

"General…" the drone operator began.

"Don't say a word," Carbonez growled through gritted teeth. He turned to the radio. "Get people out to the river. I need troops flanking, now!"

The officers replied, and through the smoke he saw a group take off as fast as they could. Grenades still sailed into the SNC ranks. The technicals, with the heaviest of the firepower—Browning .50 caliber machine guns—were hit. Two of them, at least.

Carbonez estimated the speed of his flanking group. After a minute, when the grenades stopped flying, he knew that the small group wouldn't be enough. "Send another platoon to cover them. Fast!"

Another group broke contact. In the meantime, gunners continued to lay down fire, even though they didn't have a good angle on the riverbank.

The leader of that group of shooters came over the radio. "On station at the embankment. Subjects have taken cover. Cannot make visual confirmation. Proceeding with caution."

"Backup is approaching. Wait for them to join you," Carbonez ordered.

"I see a hole in the embankment…it looks like—"

Over the radio, the screams of the patrolmen rose to a crescendo, punctuated by three thunderous booms. Mines? A sniper?

Carbonez heard more distant blasts over the radio, coinciding with a break in the haze on the live feed that showed Soldados falling or running for their lives.

Riflemen and machine gunners opened up, spraying into the smoke, trying to give cover to their injured comrades and those seeking to rescue them.

Then more bodies began to drop, struck with authority by some unseen weapon.

"What the hell is he hitting us with?" one of the Soldados called over the radio. As the man spoke, Carbonez could make out double and triple thumps of a heavy weapon. If he didn't know any better, he'd say that was the sound of an M60 or M240 light machine gun, but the bursts were too short.

Unless…

Carbonez ground his molars. "He's using a light machine gun as a precision weapon."

"What, sir?" the drone operator asked.

"Can you get the UAV lower? Under the smoke and haze? See where that muzzle flash is coming from?" Carbonez demanded.

"I'm swinging it low as it is. The mortars put too much debris into the air," the operator told him.

"It's a stolen machine. Forget about safety! Your brothers are dying down there!" the general pressed.

"It might crash into them while I can't see to steer!" the operator replied.

Carbonez trembled with rage. With shaky hands, he reached out for the man's neck, and the operator turned back, pushing the ScanEagle into a dive.

That saved the peon's life.

"He's not at the riverbank. He's somewhere in the middle. We can't see him from above. Does anyone have a muzzle flash? Anything?" Carbonez asked his troops.

"Nothing here on the ground," an officer responded. "We hear the booming of his gun, but…"

Suddenly, more fire blazed to life.

"More shooters in the smoke!" the officer shouted. "Open fire!"

A rocket slammed into the line of troops, causing more death and mayhem. The Soldados ripped off long bursts and their own rockets. "Muzzle flashes! We have muzzle flashes! Target them!"

As the officer said that, Carbonez felt his stomach drop. He slapped the drone operator's shoulder. "I need to see what's going on, now!"

"I'm getting it down to see!" the man replied.

Suddenly, instead of smoky haze, the video from the ScanEagle turned to snow and static. The operator blinked.

"What happened?" Carbonez snarled.

"The drone…went down," came the answer. "I said we shouldn't bring it down too…"

Carbonez's vision went red. A moment later, his hand was throbbing in agony, and he looked down to see the drone operator lying on the floor of the command center, head bent at a horrible angle. Blood only trickled from a laceration received on his way to the floor. His eyes remained open, unblinking.

"You…killed him," Carbonez's bodyguard, Guerro, spoke up. "You broke his neck."

"He questioned my orders," Carbonez growled. He glared at the bodyguard. "Are you questioning me?"

Guerro shook his head. "He got what was coming to him, sir."

"Good," Carbonez said. "Things have gone to shit out there. Somehow, those bastards got our people shooting *at each other*. And now, the radios are out. And it isn't because I broke them…we're just getting static."

Guerro looked as if he were about to say something but remained quiet.

That's right. You keep your mouth shut, Carbonez thought. His eyes were wide, his breathing heavy, the roar of blood loud in his ears. He knew that his temper and blood pressure had risen out of control. His rage at the impotence he now felt, at the failure of the drone and the radios, was threatening to burst blood vessels.

Suddenly, new footage came to life on the monitors. It looked like the image from their ScanEagle, but it wasn't; this drone swooped over the wreckage of the lost UAV. Everyone in the command center realized the implications of this.

"The American and the Witch had their own aerial unit," Guerro said. "They saw us coming..."

"It's how they could target the mortar trucks with such precision," Carbonez added. "And now, they're on our frequency. Maybe they always knew we were coming. That we had a drone in the sky watching them."

"Then...they know we're here. They can trace our communications, and they're using them to rub the defeat of those men into our faces," Guerro added.

Carbonez looked to his bodyguard. "If that's the case, we're done. He's taken the SNC apart. The only way out of this is to wait for him to come to us, and stop him here."

"What?"

"Take a look at the carnage out there. We sent over a hundred men. With rockets, machine guns *and artillery* to stop him. That doesn't even count two helicopters with airborne commandos, a gunship, three motorcycle teams and two SUVs full of troops," Carbonez said. "We've shown weakness on every single front."

Guerro's jaw went slack. "If we run, we'll never stop running. The only way we get out of this is to kill him."

Carbonez shook his head. "The *best* way to get out of this is to kill him. There are other ways out of this mess, but they all involve death, slavery, mutilation and other degradations."

Guerro nodded, frowning at that assessment. "The only way we get out of this is to kill him," he repeated.

Carbonez began to scowl but understood what the bodyguard was saying. To think of any possibility of defeat would be self-sabotage.

Carbonez watched his own people succumb to confusion, confronting each other as enemy forces. Unable to communicate with them, he pulled out his gun and destroyed the monitor. There was no value in seeing any more of this slaughter.

He had a war to finish.

AFTER FIRING A SALVO of buckshot rounds, the Executioner had dropped heads for long enough to rise from his foxhole with the M60 and rush along the length of the old tunnel. Just as he'd calculated, there was another hole torn in the camouflage of the ditch, and he dove into it while the Soldados continued their back and forth, shooting at each other. As of right now, with their communications thrown into disarray, the Colombian gangsters were acting in self-defense against their own, except when Bolan tore more chunks out of their numbers with the 40 mm Milkor.

Those thunderous blasts had trimmed things

down enormously. What had once been a force of a hundred and twenty to a hundred and forty Soldados had been whittled down to what Bolan estimated to be fewer than fifty men still in fighting condition. Savage explosions and precision gunfire on the Executioner's part accounted for at least forty to fifty dead and dozens more wounded. The Colombians themselves, in the mash of anger, confusion and panic, had maintained their marksmanship and taken out another two dozen of themselves.

From his new vantage point, Bolan saw that the rest of the tunnel was fairly intact all the way to the crater where the safe house had once stood. A few holes in the camouflage would give him different points to engage the enemy and then retreat to cover.

Bolan had come to Colombia with the intention of utterly annihilating Los Soldados Nuevos de Cali, and so far, his plan had been going swimmingly. But that didn't mean he could grow sloppy, trading fire with superior forces as he stood, M60 in one hand, shouting in the middle of an empty field.

That kind of foolish bravado could be left to the movies.

Groups of men continued firing and maneuvering. Some were disciplined, cutting loose with short bursts, while others leaned on the trigger and emptied their guns in one ragged discharge.

Bolan shouldered the M60 and concentrated on the professionals, tapping off two- and three-round salvos at those conserving their ammunition. Bodies struck by high-velocity rounds crumpled, the Executioner's canny marksmanship and familiarity with the machine gun allowing him to turn it into an army-destroying weapon.

The horsepower of the bullets and the precision fire through the long barrel combined to knock down Soldados as quickly as they appeared in his sights. Tri-bursts cored torsos and smashed skulls, ejecting clouds of crimson spray. Gunmen fell into heaps of mangled flesh, rapidly expiring, if not killed instantly by the powerful rounds.

When three quarters of the two-hundred-round M60 belt were spent, Bolan noticed the battlefield grow quiet. The occasional gunshot sounded, but no more weapons blazed on full auto, no more rockets flew. The Pig had feasted well, tearing through the ranks of the SNC, and few were left to fight back.

Bolan set down the M60, trading it for the more nimble, handy M4. He emerged from the foxhole, scanning for movement in the settling smoke. He hadn't gone ten yards before he saw the first of the dead, a Cali soldier who had been hit in the upper chest with a tri-burst of 7.62 mm NATO.

Once more, the close range destruction of the Pig had provided graphic evidence of its power and mastery of the battlefield. The war grounds were quiet, abandoned. Those who could walk or run had already fled the rampant destruction. The Executioner stalked along, wary for armed foes, listening for the moans of those suffering and in need of a mercy shot.

"Cooper?" Rojas called over the hands-free radio.

"Are you at the safe house?" he asked.

"I'm in the car I found there," she told him. "Your friend, the Bear, has located the headquarters of the enemy."

"So you're coming to pick me up and take me there?"

"Sorry about disobeying orders, but even halfway across town, we've been hearing things. Now, it's a lot quieter, so I figured you were done, or almost done," Rojas told him.

"Almost," Bolan returned, keeping an eye out for trouble. In case he encountered a substantial resistance, the grenade launcher on his rifle had one of the buckshot rounds in its breech, ready to spit out a wall of damnation that would peel flesh from bone. Anything less would be dealt with via a tri-burst from the M4.

"Just hang on, I'm five minutes out," Rojas said.

Bolan grunted an affirmation. "I'll make good use of the time."

"I'm bringing fresh guns and clothes, too," Rojas told him. "Need any medical assistance?"

Bolan checked himself over, but other than some bruises and a few cuts on his hands from knife work against the forward observers on the riverbank, he was in good condition.

"Disinfectant. I took a dip in the Cauca river…"

"*La caca*," Rojas said. "Pardon my pun, but that's a pretty shitty place for a swim."

"Amusing," Bolan deadpanned.

"I hope you have your shots," Rojas said.

"You'll have some boosters for me in the first aid kit."

As the words left his lips he caught a flicker of movement to his left. As Bolan began to react, the ambusher appeared.

The Soldado was blood-drenched, pieces of gore sticking to his face, but from the way he lunged, Bolan could tell he had no serious injuries. The man must have been standing too close to one of his comrades when he took a devastating hit. Bolan stepped to the side, pulling the M4 up to open fire, but the foe was swift and had a machete in hand, jolting upward and swinging the length of blackened steel down with savage velocity.

In order to keep his torso from being sliced open, the Executioner sacrificed the M4. The machete's unyielding edge slammed hard into the barrel and receiver of the carbine. The lashing machete severed the sling that bound the weapon to the warrior, but the momentum of the impact didn't tear it from Bolan's hands.

Instead of losing the rifle, he pushed forward with it. His opponent's blade was snagged in the fiberglass and metal of Bolan's weapon. With a powerful twist, he wrenched the machete from the thug's fingers, and shoved the steel collapsing stock of the carbine into the man's jaw. The crunch of cartilage was punctuated by an ugly splitting noise as the Soldado's mandible shattered.

The Colombian staggered backward half a step, fighting to stay on his feet, his carnage-soaked features twisted in rage undimmed by the blow to his jaw. The Executioner didn't pause in his counterattack, lashing out with his right leg and catching the man in his knee. Two hundred pounds of Bolan's lean, powerful might was focused behind the heel of his combat boot, obliterating the kneecap in a single kick. The Soldado toppled.

Bolan let the stunned gangster flop to the ground, taking advantage of the moment to rip his Desert Eagle from its quick-draw holster. The Executioner put his .44 Magnum right between the Colombian's eyes and pulled the trigger.

He thumbed the safety back on and slid the massive hand cannon back into its holster, hanging low on his hip.

The swift, grisly melee seemed to have been an indication to any other would-be attackers that trying one last assault against the Executioner was a futile idea. No one moved, not even when Rojas arrived, skidding to a halt at the edge of the battlefield.

Bolan strode up to the sedan and opened the passenger side door. The first aid kit was lying on the shotgun seat, so he picked it up before getting into the car.

"You look like hell," Rojas muttered.

Bolan glanced into the side mirror. Mud and dust

were caked to his face and had turned his hair a
sickly brownish gray. The mask of earth cracked
around the corners of his mouth and his eyes, where
the moisture from Cauca's rancid waters had dried.

"Might as well look the part," he said grimly.

16

It was sunset when they reached the second safe house.

"What's the plan?" Rojas asked.

Cooper said nothing as he slid his combat harness off of his shoulders, unhooking his belt and the thigh lanyard to drop forty pounds to the floor with a loud rattle. All Rojas could do was watch him peel out of his clothing. He had bruises all across his back and legs, showing where he'd hit the ground in dives for cover, or where debris launched by nearby rocket blasts had peppered him. He had no cuts, no fresh injuries, save for a few nicks on his fingers and palms from where he'd cut himself while driving his knife into the bodies of SNC commandos.

He'd wrapped those in the car with white athletic tape, but that, too, was removed and tossed aside as he climbed into the shower.

They'd decided to recharge briefly at the safe house, waiting for Carbonez to let his guard down after the latest bloody battle.

"We're going to need some food and drink," Bolan said, his voice effortlessly wafting above the hiss and spatter of the water. "I think there's something in the cupboards."

"How fancy do you want it?" Rojas asked.

"Open can, pour down throat is good enough for me," Bolan answered. "Do what you need to stomach it."

Rojas moved to the small kitchen. She'd never imagined that she'd be pulling housewife duty, but she had to admit she was hungry, too. She found some ground beef and threw it into a frying pan, mixing in pepper and spices, seasoning it as she whisked and turned it over. She poured some tomato juice into the mix, and the concoction crackled and sizzled. She added some cheese once the beef was cooked.

Rojas threw some tortillas on to a flat pan and let them brown. A little work with a head of lettuce created enough slaw for two people, and by the time Bolan emerged, fully dressed, she'd made a couple of gigantic burritos for each of them.

They didn't speak much as they ate. They were going into action again soon; Carbonez was going down, and neither Rojas nor Matt Cooper needed to give voice to that notion to believe it.

IF EUGENIO "GUERRO" DELGADO wanted to know exactly what desperation smelled like, then all he had to do was take a deep breath in the command center. The air was a cocktail of perspiration, secondhand smoke, stale beer, cold coffee and more than one bottle filled with urine. Carbonez wasn't allowing for a single bathroom break that couldn't be poured out down a sink.

Carbonez leaned on a table, puffing yet another cigarette down past the end of the filter before crushing it out on the plastic veneer of the tabletop.

Another addition to the stench of despair: hot, melted polymer.

"Hit me," Carbonez grunted, edging his mug along the table to Guerro.

"Why don't you lie down for a bit," Guerro suggested. Carbonez's cold blue eyes locked on him, as if Guerro had said something about his mother's relations with a stray dog.

"Sorry, sir," Guerro said, snatching the coffee mug off of the table and heading to the hallway for a refill.

Along the way, he passed the small office where the drone operator lay, the scent of decay setting in and spreading into the corridor like an infection. Guerro grimaced at the way his boss was coming apart at the seams. Sure, it was good thinking to stay primed and ready for the next assault. The general only had the small contingent of gunmen inside the compound left to count on. Any attempt to seek assistance from outside of the organization would be tantamount to suicide. A moment of weakness and an ounce of desperation would be all the signal a rival cartel needed to move in and take power.

There was only one thing keeping the scavengers at bay, and that was Carrillo's warning.

"Spread the word. Los Soldados de Cali Nuevos are ending. If you don't want to die alongside them, stay out of my way."

The other cartels seemed to be paying heed to that admonition. From the moment the Witch and the American had set foot in Colombia, the entire criminal underworld seemed to sense that a horrific storm was coming.

No, Guerro thought. Storms come once. They strike, and though they may rage violently, they leave eventually. This was something different, something malicious, a force of nature that seemed only to pick up steam as it continued on. The American and the Witch were unrelenting in their actions, appearing to gain strength in the face of street ambush, in the face of counterattacks, and now in the face of an entire armed force pulling out all the stops.

In the wake of over a hundred dead, adding to the dozens already lost before Carbonez's "master-stroke," Guerro wasn't feeling much confidence. Still, he had a .45 on his right hip, and there were plenty of former JUNGLA commandos present…

The men they'd sent to the safe house had been armed with the best and latest rifles and other weapons.

They'd had rocket launchers.

And mortars.

They'd survived ten minutes of mayhem. Guerro hadn't been in the command center for that; he'd been outside, listening to the war occurring downriver. The blasts of artillery shells and explosive warheads had been undercut by the hiss of automatic weapons.

In the wake of the barrage, he'd heard even *more* dramatic explosions erupting as spare mortar ammunition detonated and cooked off. The sound of gunfire had been faint, hard to notice. But Guerro could make it out. They'd sent an army to overwhelm two people, but suddenly it was all for naught. Not only had the SNC wasted valuable ammunition, but they'd now lost the very weaponry that would have fired it.

Not to mention the men. Vehicles. Not just trucks and cars and motorcycles, but aircraft, too.

Even the drone they'd snagged from the Colombian government.

Guerro filled Carbonez's mug and noticed a tremor in his hand as he put down the pot. He clenched his fist in an effort to stay the shakes, to get himself under control, but the truth was that his heart was pounding hard as he took detailed inventory of their losses for the third time tonight. He glanced up at the clock in the kitchenette and saw that it was two-thirty in the morning.

How many hours? The sun went down at nine, and Carbonez had unleashed hell at 8 p.m. The general

had even been counting on sunset to cover the approach of the attack formation. They'd fired down
on the American while backlit by the setting sun,
limiting visibility. It was a stratagem that had been
used countless times since the beginning of warfare.

And if it hadn't been for the enemy having their
own ScanEagle, as well as a solid understanding of
physics and indirect fire, it would have been an un-
stoppable assault.

Would have. Could have. Should have.

But it hadn't been.

Guerro gulped down the coffee from Carbonez's
mug. He blinked, hoping the caffeine would kick
in and reenergize him. Everything that was supposed to be sewn up airtight—Macco's security,
Herrera's unassailable livery, even the reception at
the airport—had been shown to be utterly worth-
less. Guerro couldn't help but think that this conflict
wasn't some wild-assed, on-the-fly operation. The
American and the Witch always seemed to be a step
ahead of the Soldados. Even when it seemed as if the
SNC had the upper hand, the pair was always on the
offensive, never the defensive. How could that be?

Guerro refilled the mug for his boss, anxious to
get back to the command center. Despite the stink,
he'd left his M4 there, and he realized that no handgun, even a .45 auto, was going to help match the
assault skills of their enemy.

He walked along, holding his breath against the
stench of the dead drone operator. If they didn't do

anything about the corpse, the odor of rot would fill the building from top to bottom by morning. And if the remaining Soldados kept burning through coffee at this rate, they'd run out before sunrise. Then would come the crashes.

But Carbonez wouldn't rest. He continued to watch the security cameras, constantly checking in with his men over the radio.

No one would rest.

And after the stress and anticipation of the past few days, the growing paranoia, the dread that nothing they did would work…sleep would not be coming. There was no relaxation on the horizon, unless one party or the other was lying dead on the floor.

The reek of the dead Soldado in the headquarters was not a good omen.

IT WAS FOUR in the morning, and sunrise would not be for another hour. Mack Bolan and Brunhilde Rojas were both clad in black, moving in silence.

They'd considered hanging back, peppering the office complex with grenades and shoulder-fired rockets like they'd done at the livery.

Indeed, that might seem a suitable response for Carbonez after the SNC's earlier all-out artillery assault. However, the general's headquarters were in the middle of a Cali neighborhood. Bolan wasn't willing to let even a single stray shell put innocent people at risk. No, this was going to be close combat all the way.

The Executioner and his ally had left their rifles and carbines behind, opting instead for weapons designed for close quarters mayhem. They were both armed with Mini Uzi submachine guns—deadly and reliable little chatterboxes that could rip through their thirty-two-round magazines at a rate of 950 rounds per minute.

They were also packing sidearms, and their faces and hands were blacked out with greasepaint, making them appear to any enemies as shadows come to life.

Bolan had been in a similar situation when all this started ten days ago. But things had changed since he'd discovered Teresa Blanca's body in that Texas mansion. That first mission had been a reconnaissance effort. Sadly, it had not been a rescue.

This assault was one of brutal finality. Bolan was going to make the last blitz to obliterate those who had orchestrated Teresa Blanca's death—and hundreds of others. Rojas was firmly by his side, armed and ready to fulfill her own thirst for vengeance. She'd been promised freedom for her service, but that wasn't her motivation.

Bolan knew that liberty didn't interest Rojas. And she was well aware that if she returned to being a cocaine queen, the privileges the Justice Department afforded her would disappear.

When Bolan had made Rojas get out of the sedan, excluding her from the fight at the safe house, he hadn't been protecting her. He'd sent her a message, and he was fairly certain she'd heard it loud and clear. He'd wanted her to know who was the most dangerous person on this team, wanted to remind her that although they'd accomplished a great deal together, he could have done it alone. Yet he'd chosen her as an ally and had brought her into the final battle. A person like Rojas would take that message to heart. It would keep her loyal, on his side.

Despite all that, Bolan understood that for Rojas, all of this was worth it because her son, Pepito, would be guaranteed his safety, his freedom. He would live in the United States, grow up to be an honest man, far from the shady corners of inner cities, his hands clean of blood and cocaine. Her presence at Bolan's side would ensure that no cartel would even glance sideways at her son again.

Bolan hadn't asked what Rojas would do when their crusade against the SNC was over. She knew how to survive in the hard streets, especially with her skills and savvy. There was a whole city of scum she could prey on, other criminals whom he'd all but told her were fair game. He'd warned her against harming a single civilian. Maybe, just maybe, she could make a difference, a former cocaine queen, working to save lives, not destroy them.

The office building, long ago taken over by the SNC, was ringed with video cameras, and there were sentries outside, patrolling in silence. Bolan pulled out his electromagnetic gadget and aimed at a camera. Except for the click of the activation switch, the device didn't make a sound. He scrambled each camera that came into view as they advanced.

Now, they were at a service entrance.

Bolan pulled a remote detonator from one of the pouches on his combat harness, and pressed the trigger.

In the distance, up the street and far around the corner, a series of cracks and pops erupted, duplicating the sound of an automatic weapon going off.

In moments, men were racing across the grounds in the darkness, running toward the sound of the faux-gunfire. They were all armed, and they moved with military precision and determination. These were the last of Carbonez's men, the elite, rogue soldiers he'd chosen as his personal cadre to protect both him and the SNC headquarters.

The distraction bought the Executioner vital minutes. He removed his chisel-pointed pry-knife from his battle harness and jammed it into the lock of the service door. He gave the broad handle a sharp slap, and the door jolted. The rattle was loud, and Rojas glanced back nervously, but no guards seemed to have been in earshot.

A second, then a third slap and the dead bolt gave way. Bolan sheathed the knife, gripped the Uzi, then opened the door.

"Get inside," he whispered.

Rojas did as she was told, pausing only long enough to mount a SLAM on the wall just inside the door. She tapped the controls, setting it to motion detection, and then she and Bolan moved along, heading down the corridor.

They paused at a juncture, Rojas providing cover as Bolan stuck another SLAM on the wall. With its disk-shaped explosive charge, the Selectable Light Assault Munition could spear a lance of boiling copper through a parked vehicle or function as an antipersonnel weapon, blasting out a lethal combination of force, heat and shrapnel.

Bolan drew the Desert Eagle from his hip holster, snapping off the safety with one sweep of his thumb. He opened fire on a floor tile, blasting away with four thunderous .44 Magnum roars.

It was time to bring the brave little Soldados inside, so he could slam the door shut on them.

17

As Mack Bolan and Hilde Rojas reached the stairs of the office complex, they heard the first SLAM go off.

Untroubled by the blast behind them, they slipped into the stairwell. Bolan led the way up with long strides, and he crashed open the door on the second floor landing with such violence, he caught the two guards on the other side by surprise. The door slammed into one man's face with a sickening crack and a spray of blood. The other sentry froze at the sight of the Executioner, midnight-black from head to toe except for two bright, gleaming blue eyes.

This guy was an easy target, and one that La Brujah took as she passed through the doorway in Bolan's wake. She pressed the barrel of her Mini Uzi under the surprised gangster's chin and pulled the trigger. The short tri-burst ripped away his face and split open his forehead, killing him instantly.

Bolan reached around the door, grabbing the other man by the throat with fingers like iron. The battered thug gurgled briefly before Bolan pressed the tip of his Uzi to the end of the guy's nose and let loose three 9 mm rounds.

Soldier and Witch moved up the steps, Rojas going on ahead this time, taking the stairs three at a time. Intel gathered by Stony Man had placed Carbonez and the rest of his high command on the fourth floor.

When Bolan and Rojas were between the second and third floors, guards burst into the stairwell above them. Rather than meet the Soldados on the landing, they stood their ground and fired up at the group rushing to confront them. The Colombian cartel force were making a racket as they descended, their flashlights slicing into the dimly lit stairwell and giving away each man's position. Bolan and Rojas, on the other hand, were nearly undetectable, despite the muzzle flashes and reports from their Mini Uzis.

The cartel soldiers, hoping to catch the invaders off guard, were instead overtaken by a swarm of 9 mm rounds. Two of the five men rushing into the stairwell were wearing body armor that protected them from the initial salvo of hollow points that chewed the distance between them at a velocity of over four hundred yards per second. The other three weren't as lucky, and they toppled, limp and lifeless, down the steps.

Bolan let the Mini Uzi drop on its sling, and he

pulled the .44 Magnum from his hip. He aimed the
Desert Eagle at head level, and in a moment, one of
the armored thugs lost his helmet thanks to the explosive over-penetration of two-hundred-forty grains of
Magnum power. Beside him, Rojas also transitioned
to a sidearm, pulling out the FN Five-seveN and
cutting loose with a rapid quartet of shots. The 5.7
mm rounds sliced through the other guard's Kevlar
vest. Rojas's swift staccato of sizzling lead punched
through the gunman's heart, and he slumped into
the railing, his own weight and momentum driving
him over the side.

The corpse bounced off metal on its way down,
landing at the bottom of the stairwell in a bloody,
mangled heap.

The pair paused on the next landing, quickly re-
placing spent Uzi and pistol magazines. The last
thing either of them needed was to rush into their
next conflict with empty guns. Speed was one thing.
Discipline and preparedness made their reflexes
sharper and their attacks more relentless.

Bolan finished reloading and pulled out a SLAM,
set it to motion detector mode, and placed it by the
door to the third floor. Rojas set up another on the
flight just below.

The SLAM Bolan had placed in the first floor
hallway exploded violently, and screams carried into
the stairwell. So far, they'd kept the outdoor and
ground level sentries at bay with the two antipersonnel mines.

When Bolan and Rojas reached the fourth floor, they didn't leave the stairwell right away. Instead, they quickly mounted more of the deadly munitions on either side of the door, setting them to radio detonation. They retreated up several steps, and Bolan nodded at Rojas.

"Clear them out," he whispered.

Rojas stabbed her thumb down on the detonator. The twin SLAMs went off, blasting through the drywall. Jagged shrapnel rocketed away from the holes blown by the plasma copper lances. Superheated and accelerated to bullet-like speeds, the shards of debris tore into the Soldados on the other side of the wall.

The men wearing body armor lost their arms to the scythe-like cutting force of the SLAMs and their shrapnel waves. Those without armor were dead men walking, ribs shattered, lungs perforated, aortas slashed by splinters of drywall and support studs. Screams of agony and terror erupted through the chasms blown through the walls.

Bolan pulled a hand grenade and lobbed it through one of the ugly gaps, Rojas following up for the other aperture, and they retreated to the next landing. Smoke and dust blew into the stairwell as the fragmentation bombs went off nearly in unison, silencing those left wounded and screaming after the SLAM attack.

As the dust settled, the door and its frame toppled over, collapsing into the hallway. Bolan and Rojas moved out of the stairwell, keeping an eye on their corners, knowing that even though they'd taken out at least eight men, there would be others waiting for them. There were likely another dozen former JUNGLA troopers on this floor, all armed to the teeth and on edge.

Despite the hours of standing by in fear and anticipation since the last battle, these were still military men who prided themselves on their endurance and discipline. No matter how long they waited, worried and fretted, they'd be ready for the next assault. Every ounce of doubt and fear would drain away with the surge of adrenaline that only automatic weapons fire and heavy explosions could trigger.

"Clear left," Rojas said.

Bolan didn't reply; he simply nodded, giving the former crime queen all the information she needed. He advanced to the left. Carbonez's radios and phones had been located on the north side of the building, and they were headed in that direction. Bolan paused to put a single round in a suffering gangster who rasped and rattled on the hallway floor, then he pulled a second fragmentation grenade from his harness. He thumbed the pin from the safety and rolled the mini bomb hard, like a bowler, bouncing it off the wall and sending it careening around the corner. As the deadly little pineapple-skinned bomb disappeared from sight, he heard shocked cries and the scramble of boots on linoleum. Then the fragger detonated.

The blast was Bolan and Rojas's cue to push forward, Rojas providing rear security as they turned the corner.

Bolan handed out mercy in the form of 9 mm pain pills, putting the injured Colombian guards out of their misery with shots to the head. There was a detonation in the stairwell as the remaining guards from the third floor tripped the mine.

That blast also brought up a group of gunners who rushed in to flank Bolan and Rojas. La Brujah had just enough of an opening to cut loose with her Mini Uzi, ripping into the two lead cartel commandos with lashing streams of auto fire. A third member of the ambush squad ducked low as soon as he heard gunfire, but Rojas released the trigger after her first burst, pushed the muzzle down and aimed at the prone Soldado, hammering him into the ground.

Bolan plunged forward, moving on the end of the blast, his chatterbox seeking out targets. The next thing he felt was a hammer blow that turned the world into a brilliant blaze of white. Through his protective earbuds, he heard the muffled crash of a flash-bang grenade. He hadn't been wearing polarizing goggles, but even those would barely have shielded him from the extreme luminary discharge.

But it would take lot more than a flash-bang to render the Executioner helpless. Even with his eyes clamped shut, he could hear the sizzling whistle of something coming toward him. Bolan pushed up his Uzi's frame, sacrificing the submachine gun to protect his arms and torso. Sure enough, the clash of metal on metal met his ears. A machete had crashed into his weapon.

It was a shame he was so familiar with the sound of a machete slashing his guns, he thought wryly. Based on the angle at which the blade had hit, Bolan calculated the position of the man wielding it. In one swift, smooth motion, he sidestepped and reversed the Uzi, hooking the tube-steel stock of the little sub gun around the neck of the man who had just tried to kill him.

"Get off me!" the thug snarled in Spanish before the Executioner swung hard, driving his elbow into the man's face. Bolan felt the hot spray of blood across his forearm, accompanied by the crunch of nose and facial bones. The machete clanged as it dropped to the floor, and Bolan felt his foe's legs give out beneath him. He would have finished the guy with a 9 mm slug, but after the encounter with the machete, Bolan didn't trust his Uzi anymore. He drew his Desert Eagle from his hip and fired a .44 Magnum into the Soldado's skull.

Up ahead, automatic weapons blazed. He made out the chatter of Rojas's Mini Uzi and the flashes of the Soldados M4s and handguns.

Bolan felt along the wall for a doorway, and then ducked into a small room, diving to the floor as bullets whipped over him. A blast went off in the hallway, and the floor shuddered. Rojas must have thrown another fragmentation grenade.

Bolan's vision was clearing. A Soldado stepped

past the door, on his way to join the fray, but Bolan cut him off, twin two-hundred-forty grain hollow points catching the man under his jaw, cracking open the thug's brain pan. The dead man crashed into the far wall, leaving a dark smear on the paint.

The Desert Eagle's mighty reports drew the attention of Carbonez's other surviving troops, but they expected their opponent to be on his feet. 5.56 mm rounds sawed through the wall at chest level, leaving the prone Bolan unharmed.

"How many?" Bolan said into his radio.

"There are four of them, not counting the thug you dropped," Rojas said. "They pushed me back, even with my grenade."

"That's okay, it kept me alive," Bolan responded. He rolled sideways to obtain an angle on one of the Colombian riflemen, and fired the Desert Eagle. The Executioner smashed an ugly pit into the middle of the Soldado's face, hurling him to the ground and silencing the chatter of the man's assault rifle. Bolan rolled again as bullets sliced through the wall, chewing at the section of floor he'd been lying on moments before.

Rojas's Uzi spoke up, Parabellums ripping out at nine-hundred-fifty rounds per minute. Bolan cut loose with the .44 Magnum, firing through the wall, and despite the roar of gunfire he heard another body thump to the ground. Rojas and the Executioner had put that last guy down in unison.

"Wait!" a voice shouted.

"For what?" Bolan bellowed.

"I'm out…I can't shoot back!"

"Who is this?" Bolan asked.

"My name's Guerro. My boss is down. He's hurt, and he's unarmed, too."

Bolan rose to a crouch and peered through the perforated drywall into the office on the other side of the hallway. He could make out one figure, also sitting on his heels, leaning over…something.

"Please. You wouldn't shoot someone who's hurt and defenseless, would you?" Guerro asked.

Guerro was right; he wouldn't. Even so, Bolan didn't trust the situation. Suddenly, a stench reached him—the smell of death and rot. Whatever—whoever—Guerro was leaning over had been a corpse longer than this firefight had lasted—longer, even, than Bolan and Rojas had been in the building.

Bolan dumped the spent mag in his Desert Eagle and fed it a new one. Carbonez was trying one last ruse, and the Executioner could literally smell the deception.

Rojas crouched nearby. Bolan could see her more clearly through the ragged hole in the wall.

"You're forgetting one thing, Guerro!" Rojas said. "He isn't alone. La Brujah is here!"

"Keep her away!" Guerro shouted. "Please! I'm unarmed. I didn't do shit to that spy, Blanca!"

Bolan slipped into the hall, moving behind Rojas. "Guerro says he's got an injured person there," he whispered to her.

"I recognize the rot, too," Rojas said.

"Just be ready. He might try something."

"Please, accept my surrender," Guerro pleaded.

Bolan ignored this as he crept back to an intersection of corridors they'd passed earlier. He heard the crumble of rubble beneath soles, a softly hissed curse. At least one man was sneaking up on them.

Rojas glanced back at him, and Bolan gave her the nod.

"Fuck you, Guerro!" Rojas shouted. She opened fire, blazing through the shredded office wall. Immediately, another automatic weapon opened up, but Hilde Rojas stood strong. The Uzi created a tongue of fire as she riddled the drywall.

That brought the hidden man rushing around the corner, his booted feet pounding the linoleum. Bolan pressed himself against the wall, invisible to the approaching Soldado.

Antonio Carbonez had both hands on his 1911 as he rounded the corner, obviously expecting to catch Bolan and Rojas off guard. Instead, Bolan clamped one hand around Carbonez's gun wrist, fingers digging down like steel talons and wrenching the surprised cartel leader off balance.

"No! No! I had yo—"

The Executioner blew off Carbonez's head with a single pull of the Desert Eagle's trigger, the fat .44 Magnum slug slipping between the bars of his lower mandible, punching through his tongue and stabbing up into the man's brain. The top of Carbonez's skull flipped back, torn open like a trap door; a geyser of gore sprayed the ceiling and wall behind him.

Sightless, glassy blue eyes looked at Mack Bolan for a long moment before the last vestiges of strength left the Colombian. He dropped to the ground, his career as the deadliest, most ruthless man in Cali forever ended.

"I thought you said you were going to make him beg to be killed," Rojas said, reloading her Uzi.

Bolan looked at her from the corner of his eye. "I lied. I'm not into torture. Just destroying threats and ending suffering."

Rojas looked at what was left of Antonio Carbonez, slumped on the floor. She shouldered her Uzi and opened fire, riddling the corpse with the full magazine from the submachine gun.

Bolan remained silent, waiting for her to stop.

"I know it wasn't necessary…but animals like this one killed my sons," Rojas said. "Granted, those sons did the same kind of things, the same way that he did…but I needed to get rid of the hate."

Bolan nodded. "So, are you ready to return to the States? We can't let you go back to New York City."

Rojas shook her head. "I'm staying in Cali."

Bolan tilted his head. "Not even going back for Pepito?"

"He's living a good life without me," Rojas told him. "I don't deserve to darken his life. I've got a lot to atone for."

"If you get back into…"

"I know. One slip, and you'll bring me down. And I never want to be on your bad side," Rojas said. "I'm not made out for polite society, but I can still be a bandit. The kind that fights for good."

"The other gangs and cartels in Cali will still want a piece of you..." Bolan warned.

Rojas smirked. "They'll be looking for La Brujah," she explained. "If you catch my meaning, *Cooper.*"

Bolan ignored her insinuation, though he didn't mind that she wasn't buying his alias—probably hadn't since day one. She could believe whatever she wanted about him, as long as his true identity remained a secret. "So, there will be no more wicked witch?" he asked, holding out his hand.

Rojas took it, laughing lightly at Bolan's evasion. "Goodbye, Matt Cooper."

Brunhilde Rojas's laughter was pretty, a change of pace after days of slaughter, gunfire and screams. Just the sort of soundtrack the Cali sunrise deserved as the two warriors left behind the wreckage of Los Soldados Nuevos de Cali.

* * * * *

COMING SOON FROM

GOLD EAGLE®

Available August 4, 2015

THE EXECUTIONER® #441
MURDER ISLAND – *Don Pendleton*
On an uncharted island, a psychotic hunter stalks the ultimate prey: man. His newest targets are an international arms dealer—a criminal who was in CIA custody when his plane was shot down—and Mack Bolan, the Executioner.

STONY MAN® #138
WAR TACTIC – *Don Pendleton*
Tensions between China and the Philippines are on the rise, and a series of pirate attacks on Filipino ports and vessels only makes things worse. Phoenix Force discovers that the pirates are armed with American weapons, while Able Team must hunt down the mastermind behind the attacks.

OUTLANDERS® #74
ANGEL OF DOOM – *James Axler*
The Cerberus fighters must battle Charun and Vanth, alien gods intent on opening a portal to bring their kind to earth. If the alien forces succeed, an invasion from a barbaric dimension will lay siege to Europe…and beyond.

COMING SOON FROM

GOLD EAGLE.

Available September 1, 2015

GOLD EAGLE EXECUTIONER®
SYRIAN RESCUE – *Don Pendleton*
Tasked with rescuing UN diplomats lost in the Syrian desert, Mack Bolan is in a deadly race against time—and against fighters willing to make the ultimate sacrifice.

GOLD EAGLE SUPERBOLAN®
LETHAL RISK – *Don Pendleton*
A search-and-rescue mission to recover a high-ranking defector in China leads Mack Bolan to a government-sanctioned organ-harvesting facility.

GOLD EAGLE DEATHLANDS®
CHILD OF SLAUGHTER – *James Axler*
When Doc is kidnapped by a band of marauders in what was once Nebraska, Ryan and the companions join forces with a beautiful but deadly woman with an agenda of her own…

GOLD EAGLE ROGUE ANGEL™
THE MORTALITY PRINCIPLE – *Alex Archer*
In Prague researching the legend of the Golem, archaeologist Annja Creed uncovers a string of murders that seems linked to the creature. And Annja is the next target…

CNMGE0815

Bolan crouched there for long moments, poised on the knife-edge of action. An acrid odor filled his nostrils— an animal stink. He lunged forward, rolling away.

A heavy body, tawny and striped black, slammed down on the spot where he'd been crouched. A long shape unwound and turned toward him, tail lashing in frustration as Bolan rose to his feet. He hadn't expected to see a tiger, and the microsecond of surprise that followed nearly cost him his life. The animal leaped again. Bolan jerked aside. His back slammed into a tree, and the tiger surged past, vanishing into the foliage with a frustrated snarl.

Adrenaline pumping now, Bolan tracked the flashes of orange as the animal circled him. He hefted the UMP, considering. The soldier rarely killed animals unless absolutely necessary. Then again, he might not get the chance.

As the thought crossed his mind, the tiger sprang toward him again, jaws wide. Bolan shoved himself away from the tree and began to run. He hurtled forward, the sharp edges of the plants smacking into him. He could hear the tiger panting behind him. The Executioner began calculating the distance he would need between himself and the animal to get off a good shot. If it came down to it, he would have to roll when the beast lunged and try to get under it. He might stand a chance if he could put a shot into its heart or its head before the tiger opened him up with its claws.

Suddenly, the greenery gave way to a sea of lights. Bolan skidded to a halt inches away from the wide expanse of tinted glass that marked the boundary of the rooftop atrium. The glass was wet with condensation, but even so he could see the panorama of Hong Kong at night spread out before him.

The indoor jungle was only one of the international arms dealer's endless indulgences. The tiger was another, judging by its rhinestone collar.

Bolan heard the scrape of the tiger's paws and spun, leveling the UMP. But too late. The tiger hit him like a cannonball, and he slammed backward into the glass. There was a sound like a hundred bottles shattering at once, and then the night air caught him, and he was spinning through space in a cloud of broken glass.

Don't miss
MURDER ISLAND by Don Pendleton,
available August 2015 wherever
Gold Eagle® books and ebooks are sold.

DON PENDLETON'S MACK BOLAN®

> "Sanctioned by the Oval Office, Mack Bolan's mandate is to defuse threats against Americans and to protect the innocent and powerless anywhere in the world."

This longer format series features Mack Bolan and presents action/adventure storylines with an epic sweep that includes subplots. Bolan is supported by the Stony Man Farm teams, and can elicit assistance from allies that he encounters while on mission.

Available wherever Gold Eagle® books and ebooks are sold.

GOLD EAGLE®

GESB2015